Fortress Santa Maria

General Andrew Jackson had driven the Cherokees southwards towards the sea, into Spanish territory. He was exceeding his orders, which wouldn't normally have concerned him. However, on this occasion he had a New England reporter in his army and this mysterious man threatened the general with exposure of his territorial ambitions.

Meanwhile, though, there was a bloody war to be fought and one of the bravest Indians, Black Hawk, proved to be a thorn in the side of the infantry. But at last he was captured and promised a speedy death by the bloodthirsty general.

Did the Indian chief have a hope in hell of escaping the rope? Who was the mysterious reporter? These and many more questions have to be answered before peace returns to the country.

Fortress Santa Maria

Philip Cornwell

A Black Horse Western

ROBERT HALE · LONDON

© 1953, 2003 Gordon Landsborough
First hardcover edition 2003
Originally published in paperback as
Lone Cherokee by Mike M'Cracken

ISBN 0 7090 7315 1

Robert Hale Limited
Clerkenwell House
Clerkenwell Green
London EC1R 0HT

Typeset by
Derek Doyle & Associates, Liverpool.
Printed and bound in Great Britain by
Antony Rowe Limited, Wiltshire

1

THE HORSEMAN!

Danger sent the nearly-naked Indian chief pulling back on the rope halter of that big, sweating horse that had been won in battle with the United States' cavalry.

He saw their peril the moment he came on top of that sheer-sided bluff, which rose in solitary majesty out of the lush green vegetation of this near-tropical territory of Florida. He saw those advancing columns – to the north, to the east and to the west. Saw the blue uniforms that had hounded and harried them this last six weeks, driving them ever nearer to the sea beyond which there was no escape.

And they were close, closer than he had expected.

The sudden jerk on the horse's head made it rear, though half-heartedly, because of the weariness in those great, long legs. There was war-paint on it – the

5

war-paint that had been applied with such fierce hopes so recently. There were big orange circles painted on its flanks and around the beast's eyes, and there were crosses, all designed to give it a frightening aspect.

Yet it had frightened no one. Certainly it hadn't frightened these militia or their general, Andrew Jackson, who had tracked them so relentlessly.

Chief Red Wolf knew now they were near to their end.

His horse nearly went backwards into space over the edge of the bluff, and Red Wolf brought it away from that danger in the manner of a man who wasn't too concerned if death did rise up to take him that way.

He looked down at his people below, men and women of the Cherokee tribe, and his tired eyes were filled with the tragedy he knew was inevitable. He saw two hundred men, women and children – the two hundred who had survived those long days of fighting, and the agony of their struggle through the fetid swamps of this land foreign to them.

They were lying on the ground, exhausted. Even his warriors, spent by days in the saddle and the swift, savage fighting that went with it, were squatting, their heads bent in attitudes of exhaustion. Red Wolf's eyes grieved, for he saw there was little fight left among these remnants of what had once been a great tribe.

Hopelessly his eyes turned southward, narrowing

because the sun was high and fiercely blazing into his bold, strong face. He saw that vast tree-covered plain, and then, beyond, the tropical forest which marked yet another belt of stinking, treacherous swamp-land.

He sighed. Within those Everglades there would be temporary safety for his people, but he measured the distance across the plain up to where the swamps began, and he knew that his people would never make it. The militia would catch up with them long before their tired limbs could take them to safety, and then . . .

Then there would be slaughter, an end to the Cherokees. These militia from the northlands had found this campaign harder than they had expected, and they would be savage in their retribution, in consequence.

For their leader was this celebrated Indian fighter, General Jackson, who used to say, 'The only good Injun's a dead 'un!'

Red Wolf sent his gallant black sliding down the steep slope in a flurry of dust and stones. His people looked up at him with hopeless eyes. There was even one who looked at him savagely, as if blaming their chief for this plight they were in.

Red Wolf didn't dismount. The time was too urgent to dismount.

'O People,' he called, 'we have no more time for resting. The Blue Shirts are but the distance of a running cow from us, and they are spread out, and if we stay they will come round like the horns of a

7

buffalo and we shall be trapped between the points.'

His voice urged them on to their feet. They must force their limbs into further flight, he told them.

But it was hopeless, and it seemed that all in one moment everyone knew it. Flight was impossible, with wounded among them, and women with their babes and children.

All at once every eye came round to meet Red Wolf's, and in them he read their decision.

Forked Tongue spoke what was in their minds. He had been wanting to do so for many days now, and there was malice in his voice. He was a man who had once been celebrated at the councils, and had been used in dealings with the white man. The cunning of his speech had been thought a match for the double-dealing paleface, but in time they had found he had done them no good. Now he was a discredited man, and he smarted because he no longer was listened to at the council fire.

'We have no strength. We cannot go on. Here we must die!'

Forked Tongue gestured towards the yellow sand-hills within which they rested. And his savage eyes told the chief, 'This is your fault! Our blood is upon your head!'

Red Wolf ignored that look and gesture, though he was no fool and could read what was in Forked Tongue's mind. This was no time for squabbling among themselves. He addressed his people again. He asked, 'Is that in your minds, that you cannot go on?'

Big, good-tempered Running Elk spoke up, as he always spoke up at tribal pow-wows. 'That is in our mind, O Chief. Most are without horses, and the strength has left our bones. Our womenfolk must have time if they are to traverse the plain and gain the safety of the land-which-is-mostly-water.'

Red Wolf sighed. Then his shoulders shrugged. He had been dreading this moment, but he had known for these past hours that it must come. The human frame could stand just so much, and then it gave in.

'Then there is only one thing we warriors can do,' he told them, and his voice was harsh because he knew he was talking of death for most of them. 'Time must be given for our weaker ones to gain the safety of the swamp country.'

His eyes flickered from one stolid face to another.

'We can give them time one way only. And that way is for our warriors to turn about now and march towards the enemy and fight him and not let him pass until the sun is down. In that time, surely your weary limbs will have found strength to march into safety.'

A woman wailed and a child grew frightened and began to cry. Then Running Elk nodded. 'That is the only way,' he said. 'I am tired of running from these loud-voiced white men. I shall be glad to ride back to them, my spear in my hand and my war club ready for when my spear is useless. Let us go forth to meet them, O Chief!'

There was a tired murmur of approval from the

warriors who were with that party, but the womenfolk and the wounded were silent. They dreaded this decision, for they knew with the parting they might never see each other again.

From his horse Red Wolf looked down upon them, and he was proud to be a Cherokee and a chief over these people.

His eyes flickered to where his daughter sat apart from his people. She met his gaze and even smiled at him and then he felt that his heart would break. Because be loved his daughter and he didn't want to ride away from her. As his eyes moved away from where she sat, there was a little movement in the coarse grasses which flourished in these unusual sandhills in the Savannah lands of mid-Florida.

A man was within feet of the Indian chief's daughter. And he was a white man. But Red Wolf failed to see him.

Red Wolf's eyes looked from one face to another and then he found the hot, angry gaze of Forked Tongue glaring up at him. Forked Tongue knew that his face was betraying his thoughts, and he sought in the speech of his forked tongue to justify what was in his mind.

He shouted, 'O Warriors, this has come to us because we heeded Red Wolf, and the counsels of wiser men were ignored. Did we not say at the War Council, those many weeks ago, that we should put our trust in more talks with the white man? Did we not oppose this plan to resist them when they came to move us over the Mighty River?' His hand waved westwards to where the great Mississippi rolled far beyond their sight.

Running Elk was loyal and faithful to the chief they had followed. He came striding forward now, a big shambling Indian, but a man with a great heart. His eyes flashed scorn upon the men who preferred words to weapons.

He said, 'O thou Forked Tongue, at the council fire your tongue spoke two ways at once, so that we did not know what you were advising. No, I say that we did right in coming to this decision, even now. I say it is right, even though we were not successful in resisting the advance of the American soldiers, and now we are faced with a battle that will surely wipe the Cherokee nation off the face of the earth.'

His eyes flickered to where the women and children and wounded were huddled together and he said softly. 'That is, all except our women and children who must be given chance to escape this fate.'

There was a murmur of approval from the tired but loyal warriors of Red Wolf. They had approved the war council's decision, and were prepared to accept responsibility for all that had followed.

Red Wolf's eyes were scornful as they looked at the man who had long coveted his position as chief of this tribe. He said contemptuously: 'For too long we have trusted the white man. Always he has broken his promises, until we grew tired of hearing more and we thought to stay him with our weapons because words

11

had proved useless against him.' His head sank upon his chest. His voice was weary now, and yet his eyes were steadfast, certain that what he had done had been rightly done.

'We took the right decision, to refuse to leave our lands. Because of that the white man has shown us no mercy. When he came and drove us from our hunting grounds he was not satisfied to do just that.' His hand waved to the hill beyond which the advancing American soldiers were. 'They have hounded us like prairie dogs after a lame buffalo. Now they are not content with our lands; now, our lives must go with our hunting grounds!'

And they knew he was right, but Forked Tongue wanted to pour his wrath upon a man whom he had secretly hated these many years. Because Red Wolf was a fine man and respected, and he, Forked Tongue, was watched with suspicion and no respect by his kinsfolk.

Red Wolf finally stopped his torrent of abuse. The chief's face was cold. He said, 'We have no time to fight with words among ourselves. Let the wounded, the old, the women and our children take the trail and go southward. Let them go where we were going, to the Southern Lake where the Creek Indians and the Seminoles are gathered in strength. There will be safety.'

His eyes went back to Forked Tongue's anger-blackened face. 'You, O Forked Tongue, will go with that party.'

Forked Tongue leapt like lightning towards that mighty chief upon his horse. This was a deadly insult, to put him, a warrior, with the women and children, and the aged and wounded. He had no heart for a battle with the Blue Shirts, but his fierce temper would not suffer this insult, even though it gave him a chance to escape with his life.

His hand came swinging up with his war club, and he jumped and caught Red Wolf by the naked shoulder, and in the same movement, as Red Wolf began to slip from the sweat-slippery back of his stallion, that club came whipping over to smash the life out of the chieftain.

There was a man there who had but little speech upon his lips at any time, and in consequence he seemed to have the more energy for action. He was one of the younger braves, tall, and sinewy and with a stamina that was the admiration of all other warriors.

He had seemed as tired as the other braves, but now, in this moment when his chief's life was threatened, he seemed to find strength from somewhere; for he came leaping forward and seized Forked Tongue by the wrist that held the club – and Forked Tongue found himself thrown violently on to the ground.

Red Wolf straightened and sat upon his horse again, and his eyes showed his thanks though his lips said nothing of it to the young warrior.

Forked Tongue came bounding to his feet, his face

13

savage because his pride had been humbled. He saw that younger man, and in his fury he came streaking in, his tomahawk swinging.

The young nearly-naked Indian jumped like lightning to meet his adversary, and with a shock their sweaty, naked bodies clashed together. But it was Forked Tongue who went down again, and so violent was the throw this time that he was dazed and it took him seconds to get to his feet now, and then he looked inexpressively sick.

By this time the other warriors had sprung between the contestants. There was Running Elk and Black Bear, who shouted, 'This is no time for fighting among ourselves. Keep your strength for the paleface!'

Forked Tongue climbed slowly up from the hot yellow sand. His face was white with passion, and there was a venom in his eyes when he turned to look at Black Hawk, who had struck him down. But he didn't attempt to resume the battle. He had felt the strength in that mighty young warrior's grip, and he knew that he hadn't a similar strength in his own weary muscles.

Red Wolf was giving orders now, as if there had been no sudden, murderous interlude. Back among those coarse grasses the lone spectator listened and watched, and then he began to slide back on his belly, grimly hugging the ground and taking advantage of every piece of cover available. And they were so tired, these Cherokees who had once been the most vigilant of Indian tribes, that they never saw the white man's departure.

Red Wolf was telling them of what he had seen from the top of this bluff, here in the flat lands of Florida. He had seen the Southern Lake, of which they had heard from other tribes but which until now their eyes had never rested upon. It had been far away in the distance, a blue, shimmering, sun-reflecting expanse which went out to meet the curving horizon. But he told them of something else he had seen. Right on the edge of that sea, which the palefaces called the Gulf of Mexico, was a white fortress.

That had been plain to his sharp eyes when he had sat high up on the summit of this bluff. He had seen the thick 'dobe walls with the castellated roof, and he had known it for a Spanish fortress.

He told them to keep always to the west of that fortress, because the Spaniards were, if anything, more brutal to Indians than the American white men. And then he told them to go.

He called his braves together and they came at once, leading their jaded horses. The wounded and the womenfolk turned and began to trek out of the sand hills, their faces towards the sun and the south and the treacherous, deadly swamp-lands, ten miles ahead of them.

When he saw them on their weary way, Chief Red Wolf turned his tired horse and walked it round the base of that high cliff. His warriors mounted and came at a walk behind him. In all he had less than a hundred and twenty men to face those armies of the American general. They walked their horses slowly, deliberately, into view of the distant columns of marching men. Where before they had sought to escape detection, now they wished to bring all eyes upon themselves.

When they had ridden a mile, they stopped and dismounted where there was a stream to slake the thirst of their gallant horses. It was at this time that one of the braves, looking back perhaps to see their departing kinsfolk, suddenly cried out and pointed.

They all turned, following the direction of his pointing finger.

A lone horseman was riding southward, and they felt he was keeping pace with their helpless brethren.

2

THE PRISONER!

Red Wolf's eyes grew fierce. They heard him exclaim,
'Where did he come from?'

But the next moment on everyone's mind was,
'Who is that man?'

For he was not a soldier, and he didn't have the
appearance of a Spaniard from one of the coastal
towns. And those were the only white men they
expected to see in this land of Florida which still
belonged to the Spanish Crown.

But – there was no time to consider the questions,
and no time even to think about them a second
longer. For now the military had seen them and were
closing rapidly in upon them.

They could see the troops of cavalry detaching
themselves from the marching infantry, and coming
at mad gallop over the rough country on three sides
of them. The dust was rising where horses pounded

their hoofs, and where the columns of marching men stirred the dry top soil into clouds of dust which rose even above their heads. Far in the background came the wagons, their canvas tops rocking as they came over the trackless waste.

Red Wolf gave the order to remount. When they were mounted he gave an order that surprised them.

He told them to split up into small groups, some to ride to engage the west flank and others the centre force, while he would ride with the smallest group to engage the force riding in from the east. Those braves looked at him, because in dividing their small force, he seemed to be throwing away any chance of strong resistance.

But he was a wise chief, and they obeyed him, because always until now his strategy had proved beyond the reproach of his followers. Black Hawk rode with the strongest party which went to engage the main column advancing directly from the north. He saw little of the fighting which followed on either flank, but he knew that his Cherokee brothers that day distinguished themselves and fought against odds that were overwhelming – and held their own while the heat went slowly out of that descending sun.

He saw the militia, armed with those deadly rifles of theirs, marching through the brush and between the frequent trees on that undulating plain. A minor chieftain named Tall Bush led them into battle, and he led them well. When the American cavalry came into view over a short hill right ahead of them, he gave the order to charge before the white men knew they were so near to the Indians.

In a moment those forces had clashed, and because the United States' infantry was still a mile to the rear of their cavalry their forces were nearly equal.

Black Hawk fought like the lion his chief had demanded of him. He raged like a prairie fire among those heavy white men on their massive horses, fury and desperation seeming to throw away the weariness of these days of pursuit and hardship. There was a crash of guns, and the clash of metal upon metal. Men swore and shouted and hacked and parried, and horses reared and lashed out and screamed because horses are no lovers of fighting.

There was a mighty confusion of noise and movement, and powder-smoke came drifting across into their nostrils. Everywhere nearly-naked red men engaged the blue-shirted United States' cavalry, and when they were at close quarters they were superior to the white man.

There came a time in fact when the ferocity of this small group of Indian warriors proved too much for the cavalry commander. He saw with sudden alarm that his men were in danger of being wiped out, and he regretted the impetuosity with which he had gone into the attack.

Now it was the cavalry's turn to retreat. But the Indians didn't follow them. They weren't going to ride on to the guns of the bigger force of infantry, marching as fast as they could, so near to them now.

Tall Bush gave a call and began to trot away, and his men fell in behind him. Fifteen only had survived that battle in their little group. They looked east and west of them, but there was no sign of fighting. Either it was all over, or it was being conducted in some hollow out of sight.

Black Hawk came alongside Tall Bush and they talked, because though Black Hawk wasn't a chief he was respected as a fighting man. Tall Bush said grimly, 'That was victory. They didn't expect such fighting as that.'

Black Hawk nodded. 'It was victory,' he agreed. Then his hand gestured towards their few remaining followers. 'But what is left out of the victory for us?' he demanded.

Tall Bush said: 'It will hold them back, though. Their cavalry suffered almost as much as we did, and they come cautiously when they are short of cavalry.'

Black Hawk nodded, his eyes watching the cavalry who had dismounted and were now surrounded by infantry. He said: 'Now we can worry them. All the time we can move around the infantry and fire upon them and hold them back.'

It meant that they had to split up again, and it became a case of every man for himself.

Black Hawk rode to the summit of a small mound where bushes grew thickly, almost to the height of his waist when he was seated on that weary mount of his.

He watched the distant force of battered cavalry and infantry as they regrouped for a fresh assault upon their illusive enemy. As he watched he saw the infantry begin to string out in a long line over the broken country, with the cavalry riding as a group to their rear as a reserve force, in case they were needed. The infantry's tactics were clear to the young Indian. They were going to drive their way forward, taking any Indians with them en route. It rather upset their plan to harry a marching body of men, so Black Hawk suddenly slipped from his horse and patted it and let it trot away for a few yards because it wouldn't be much use to him now.

He went into the cover of those bushes, and when he saw a movement within reach, a swift arrow sped out and found a target. The sweating militia men turned at once, their guns lifting and blasting towards him. But he was down on the ground, and those vicious bullets only chipped twigs and branches off the trees and bushes around him. Then, like a slippery snake, Black Hawk worked his way off that mound and into cover immediately behind it, so that when those militia men rushed the place – they found it deserted.

All that afternoon Black Hawk repeated his strategy. He went into hiding and fired upon an enemy who grew increasingly exasperated and yet, because of the deadliness of his aim, became more and more cautious. And every time his arrows had found a target, immediately Black Hawk would disappear from that point and reappear many yards away, to worry them again.

Sometimes he caught glimpses of his red brothers, and he could see that they too were pursuing the same tactics.

Black Hawk fought with increasing recklessness. He could hear the gruff-shouted commands of the sergeants in charge of these militia, and the orders rapped out by officers who wheeled their horses from one vantage place to another. He saw men at such close quarters that he could remember their faces ever afterwards. And he fired whenever he could and did what damage he was able.

In particular he aimed at a man who seemed careless of danger. He was an infantryman, a broad-shouldered, red-haired man with a sweating red face. A young man, and with intelligence on his face. He was reckless, this infantryman, but in some curious way his very recklessness gave him a charmed life. When Black Hawk fired on him, it was as if the Great Spirit turned the arrows away from him; for none hit, and that big, young infantryman was alive long after he should have been dead.

And then they got Black Hawk. It was an hour before sunset, with the shadows long and the heat already much departed from that great, red raging sun over the western forests. By this time they knew they had won, these few Cherokee warriors who remained to realize it. They knew that by now the enemy, no matter how fast they went, could not catch

22

up with those remnants of the once-mighty Cherokee tribe that night.

Perhaps with this realization Black Hawk allowed weariness to come to cloud his instinct for self-preservation. At any rate, he stayed too long in one position and found himself over-run. Some cavalry, emboldened because there were no Indian tribesmen mounted to oppose them, came dashing through where Black Hawk's comrades should have been, but were not. And Black Hawk found himself with blood-thirsty cavalrymen rearing their horses right behind him, covering any attempt to escape as before.

He came leaping to his feet, determined to sell his life dearly, because that way he was helping the red people. He saw horses rearing their hoofs flailing the air. He saw blue-uniformed men leaning from their saddles, their faces savage because this was a moment they had waited for. And he caught the gleam of sabres as they swung in the air.

They were crashing down upon him, five of them, all determined to be the one to put an end to that solitary Indian warrior's life. And he had so little strength left that he could hardly lift the war club which was now his only weapon, at close quarters.

They were rearing above him, about to crash down and end a life that hadn't been long begun. And then suddenly something crashed into Black Hawk's back, and he found himself sprawling among the hoofs of those horses. There was an intolerable weight upon him and the breath went clean out of his body because of it.

In the agony of returning breath, Black Hawk twisted his head and peered through the sweat that wetted his eyelashes together. He tried to struggle, but even now even his stamina had all gone.

He looked up and found himself gazing into the face of that big young infantryman with the hot sweating face and the red ruffled hair that was without infantry cap. He saw blue eyes, and they seemed as desperate as his own must have been. And yet he sensed that the desperation did not come of fear.

A mighty grip had Black Hawk pinioned by the arms behind his back. He was at a disadvantage, and, anyway, he no longer had the will to live.

There was dust kicking up and getting into his face and making him choke, where the stamping hoofs of those five cavalry horses pounded the dry top soil. There were rough, angry shouts from the men in their saddles.

'Get away there!'

'Goldarn it, let me get my sword into his guts!'

They were shouting in fury at this big, red-haired man who lay on top of the Indian and was between him and their sword points.

Black Hawk felt a tremor run through his arms, as that big-chested infantrynan shouted back at the cavalry in a voice of thunder: 'General Jackson's orders! We've got to take some prisoners!'

Black Hawk knew little of the white man's

language, yet he understood what was being shouted between that lone, kneeling infantryman, gripping him so painfully behind his back, and those milling, ferocious cavalrymen who could think only of blood.

Black Hawk found himself suddenly hoisted to his feet, and he was a big man himself, and he marvelled at the strength of this infantryman who could throw him around as if he were a reed.

He had no strength left to resist, but he had a feeling that even if he had been fresh he could not have matched this northerner in physical combat.

He found himself being dragged away from those cavalrymen, and he realized that he was being hustled towards where last he had seen the enemy's wagon trains. The cavalry for a few moments argued and began to follow, and it seemed as if they were going to take matters into their own hands.

But then they heard again the name of the general in charge of this foray and they seemed to acquire discretion, and they turned and went thundering southward now in pursuit of those womenfolk whom they had known to be with the Cherokee warriors. But they were back within half an hour with a story that the delay had saved those weaker ones of the tribe and they had escaped.

But one Indian was in their midst, and he was alive, though he wished he wasn't.

To that brave, gallant young Indian to be taken alive was in fact a shameful thing, and he would rather have fallen in the fighting and received, to his mind, the honourable death that comes in battle. Black Hawk was tied up, and the hands that did the tying were rough. Then he was thrown alongside a wagon, where the sun still beat upon him and added to a thirst that had developed all during that afternoon. And for a long time no one came near him.

In that time he heard a conversation. An officer came striding by to get some food, and his stride hesitated when his eyes fell upon the prisoner. Black Hawk looked upon a thin face with a drooping moustache that curled on either side of a small mouth. The officer shouted, and a sergeant ran up and saluted.

And Black Hawk heard that officer say, 'Who took this Indian prisoner?'

The sergeant looked at the officer, and there was surprise on his face, and then he said, 'It was an order from General Jackson, sir.'

The officer made an impatient gesture. 'Jackson never gave any orders to take Injuns prisoner,' he rapped.

The sergeant didn't know what to do, and said something about someone making a mistake. That officer made an impatient sound with his mouth, and then remembered that he was hungry and walked off quickly. He would take up this matter later.

When they were all eating, someone pushed a cup of water into Black Hawk's mouth. When he lifted his eyes after drinking gratefully, he saw that red, sweating face of the red-haired young man.

And he saw there was kindness in those eyes.

3

ESCAPE!

That long, sallow face lifted and those steely blue eyes looked at the infantryman and the general said coldly, 'You know I could get you shot for this?'

A silence for a moment in that lamp-lit tent. There was little in the way of furniture, an ammunition-box serving for a table and a smaller box for a chair for that officer upon whose face the lamp-light fell.

That officer straightened as well as his weary limbs would permit. He was in full uniform despite the weather and his arduous exertions of the day. He was as lean and hard as an old stick, and that infantryman watching him thought that he was well-named by his friends. Old Hickory was an apt nick-name.

Then the infantryman spoke, and his voice was as tough as that of the officer opposite him. His grey eyes didn't flinch at the threat, though he knew that this officer was capable of carrying it out. He said, 'Why don't you, then?'

The officer didn't answer, but his eyes looked coldly at the younger man and dared him to speak on. He was not a man who brooked insubordination.

That infantryman said levelly, 'I'll tell you why you daren't shoot me out of hand. Because there'd be a big row after this filibustering exploit of yours, more than you'd bargained for. You have marched your troops, general, into a land which does not yet belong to the United States. Florida is part of the Spanish empire, and when the Spaniards know you have invaded their territory – especially when they know it has been done without the knowledge of the United States' Government – there's going to be an international situation. Maybe there's even going to be war between those two countries.'

General Andrew Jackson, the man who was destined one day to become President of the United States, said, 'I came after rebellious Cherokee Indians. If these Spaniards harbour them and supply them with arms to fight against my people, I'll drive them all into the sea!' There was a hard finality about his statements. They were the statements of a man sure that what he does is right.

He said, 'When you joined me back at Tesca, I said you could come with my army so long as you behaved yourself. In fact, I only gave you permission so long as you joined as a volunteer infantryman. That didn't give you any rights. Yet when I rode into camp this evening I was told that you had saved the life of an Indian upon my word.' He shook his head angrily. 'I never said that any Injuns should be taken prisoner, and I won't allow any men to go around putting such statements in my mouth.'

If there had been any onlookers they would have thought it curious that a general should be faced so resolutely by the lowest in his command.

But this infantryman wasn't quite an ordinary man. Though he marched with the men, he did it in the course of another duty. For he had been sent south by a New England newspaper to investigate the Indian troubles in Georgia and Tennessee. General Jackson was afraid of no man, but he had a respect for newspapers which could ruin the reputation of a politically ambitious man – himself.

The newspaper man said coldly, 'What good does it do to kill unnecessarily?'

General Jackson said, 'To have killed that Injun wouldn't have been unnecessary. It would teach others a lesson – the power of the white man.'

That reporter looked at him and slowly shook his head. Then, in a voice that was grating, the infantry-man said to the general, 'You're kidding yourself. Killing that Indian would not have acted as a lesson to anyone.' His head shook slowly, positively. 'So many Indians have been killed in the past weeks that another Indian's death wouldn't mean a thing. That's why I jumped in and saved his life. It wasn't to anybody's advantage to kill him, and he was a brave man, prepared to give his life to save his people.'

General Jackson got to his feet. They could hear the sound of horses' hoofs approaching through the night – many of them. And there was a mighty rumble of wheels, and the shouting of men who hailed the camp fires as a haven of rest after a day's toil across those trackless wastes. The general wanted to go out to greet the newcomers.

He said brusquely, 'He dies just as soon as I can get someone to put a rope round his neck.' His tone was cold and inflexible. General Jackson was on a campaign that wasn't helped by taking prisoners.

The infantryman looked at the general and said, 'All this will go into my paper when I can get news back to let them know what is happening here in Florida.'

Jackson said, 'Print it and be damned!'

He started to go out of the tent, a lean hard angular figure. The infantryman watched him go, and then he called out, 'What's going to happen to me?'

The general turned in the doorway and the light fell upon his sweating face. His eyes looked at the dishevelled figure of the big, strong young infantryman, and then he said contemptuously, 'Be danmed to you, too!'

Jackson strode off into the darkness. The infantryman came to the tent flap and looked out. There was a small crescent moon which gave some light, and the cloudless Florida sky was studded with stars which gave added illumination.

He saw the lines of fires where the troops were bivouacked, and he saw the tents that had gone up, and the wagons were lined up neatly in military fashion. He looked beyond the fires and saw the head of a column creeping into the camp.

Firelight fell redly upon officers riding in a small group on weary, sweat-lathered, trail-dusty horses. Behind them came the more powerful horses used for pulling the guns. And there were many such teams, and the eyes of the New England reporter widened when he saw them.

Jackson's excuse that he had invaded Spanish Florida in pursuit of warring American Indians, didn't hold good now. Now it was obvious to that big infantryman that Jackson had had this invasion long-planned. Otherwise, why bring in artillery? Artillery wasn't needed against a bunch of fleeing Indians.

He moved away, his head drooping, and he was thinking. They're an excuse: all the time Jackson's idea has been to drive on to the Spanish ports and take this land for America.

It wasn't comfortable lying against that wagon, but Black Hawk was a stoic and never showed the discomfort of being so tightly bound and held immobile at a time when his weary limbs wanted movement to restore circulation. He was hungry, too, and the smell of cooking meat wafted to his nostrils and made his mouth water. But he lay there in silence, and he had his thoughts and they weren't pleasant.

He was lying there with the firelight on him, and upon the wooden spokes of that iron-rimmed wheel against which he lay, when his sharp ears caught a stealthy movement from under the wagon. He became rigid instantly. He had the sense not to turn his head, in case a quick movement attracted attention from the soldiers walking about the camp. He lay where he was and waited till he felt someone fumbling in his hair.

It was the only handgrip available to whoever was trying to rescue him, then. He wore no clothes, and his skin was smooth and slippery, and he was lying on his bound hands so that they couldn't be gripped. He felt those fingers tighten into his war-lock, and then there came the pain as someone slowly began to drag him under the wagon by means of his hair.

Black Hawk didn't cry out. An Indian didn't cry out for little pain, and what was this discomfort if it meant an escape with his life. He felt himself being slowly, carefully, dragged into the shadow under the wagon, where the firelight was hidden from them by a dropped tail-board. Then swiftly he was turned on to his face and a keen knife snicked through his bonds – and be found himself free.

There was that intolerable agony of returning circulation, but it was as nothing to the young Indian who lusted in the glory of freedom when he had thought that death was his lot for certain. He lifted his head, but saw only a shadowy form in the darkness under this wagon. He began to lift himself on to his knees, and then he felt a light touch on his shoulder and knew that he was being told to follow.

Deliberately Black Hawk came up alongside that shadowy figure, crouched ready to sprint across to the next line of wagons. He let his body touch that other shadowed body, and his bare skin felt cloth – woven material – and he knew this was a white man who had come to his rescue, and not his Indian friends. He could think of only one paleface who might do it. He had a mental picture of that big, sweating, red-haired, red-faced infantryman who had brought him water – a soldier with compassion in his eyes. He couldn't understand it. For that same infantryman had taken him prisoner . . .

He caught a whisper from the New Englander. The infantryman said softly, 'Run for it, my red brother. I will walk up towards those soldiers, and perhaps they will not notice you crossing this open lane behind my back.'

Then Black Hawk felt his hand gripped, and knew it was a way of saying good luck. He returned the pressure, but didn't say anything.

The infantryman straightened and walked up the lane towards the other soldiers. Black Hawk hesitated a second, and then flitted silently on his moccasined feet towards those other wagons. He gained their shelter and no one raised an alarm. He was well on his way to freedom now, he thought.

There were two more lines of vehicles, but with each the firelight behind became less able to penetrate the darkness, and he could move with greater freedom in consequence.

Black Hawk gained the last line of wagons, and then there were only the sentries, posted in a wide circle around the camp, to evade. Black Hawk looked out into the darkness and he had no fear. He knew that if he were given time to exercise his craft as a stalker he could pass any American soldier-sentry without being detected. But he needed time . . .

Black Hawk didn't know it, but it was at that moment that three men went towards a wagon where an unwanted prisoner had been placed. One carried a rope in his hand. They walked quickly, like men who wanted to be done with something, so they could get back to their tents and blankets – and sleep.

Black Hawk heard a man's voice bellowing an alarm from the wagons behind him, and he knew that his escape had been detected. He knew that now the camp would be alarmed, and men would come rushing to search among the wagons and wherever an escaping prisoner might be expected to hide.

He came to his knees, determined now to make a dash for the darkness beyond. He had seen the position of the nearest sentries, and there was a possibility that if he kept low as he ran he might be screened from their rifles until he was right between them.

He had almost begun that hazardous, suicidal dash over fairly open ground towards the perimeter of the camp where the sentries, now vigilant, patrolled. And then those men at the end of the first lane got the gun-carriages limbering round behind the wagon lines, and Black Hawk's startled gaze saw powerful teams of horses dragging swaying guns come wheeling down the line towards him.

His hands clenched. Fate, it seemed, had conspired to prevent his escape. Now, between him and freedom stood not only the sentries, but these plunging teams of horses and their artillerymen.

Desperately he glanced behind him. He saw forms moving in the lane right behind him, and they were within thirty or forty yards of his hiding place. Within a minute or so the search would have come up to him and he would be detected.

So he crouched, and the first of half-a-dozen guns suddenly came crashing right in front of him. The artillerymen came leaping off as soon as it halted, and they took with them their rifles. It was evident that they had been given orders, first to wheel their guns into position and then to go and reinforce the sentries around the edge of the camp.

Black Hawk heard the rough, angry talk of men as they came stamping up the ranks of wagons, their guns pointing into the shadows, ready to shoot when they saw a sign of movement. They were within fifteen yards of him now.

The horses attached to that first gun team were within five yards of him. The stink of sweating horse-flesh came pungently to his keen nostrils, and he could even see the quivering of their skins as they tossed their heads and blew through their nostrils and tried to find relief in their harness after this long, hard day dragging the gun.

There was one man ostensibly in charge of each gun team, but in fact these men had grouped together, their rifles ready, watching for the moment when, as they expected, a solitary Indian broke from cover and tried to find safety across this open ground behind the wagon lines.

Black Hawk did nothing of the kind. Like lightning he moved. He was out from under those wagon wheels like a flash, and under the belly of the nearest horse in that gun limber. They didn't move when he came up between the leading pair of horses, and lithely he swung on to the solitary wooden shaft to which team were attached.

In an instant he was crouching, balanced on that bar, his hands gripping the manes of the horses on either side of him.

Suddenly Black Hawk screamed, and it was the wild, unearthly scream that was the war cry of his people. It was too much for those horses, whose ears were within half-a-yard of his mouth.

They seemed to be crazy, and leapt into their harness, terrified and wanting only to escape from this crouching, yelling thing, so near to their heads, and so terrifying in the noise it made.

The four horses went leaping forward, the gun carriage bumping crazily behind them. Instantly there was an uproar from all the men around the camp. They shouted and pointed and it was evident that someone had spotted the glistening, naked body of Black Hawk, clinging to those gun-horses.

But Black Hawk was well covered by the bodies of those beasts, and he was whooping madly and adding to the terror of those frantic horses.

The gun and its team crashed a pathway towards the gathering line of men encircling the camp. They saw it looming out of the night, four maddened, terrified horses, with the fierce face of a nearly naked Indian crouched on the limber bar between them.

They saw a gun leaping crazily as it bounced from every undulation and threatening to overturn any second.

Startled men saw the crazily-charging gun-team, and some of them opened fire, but Black Hawk escaped without harm. And then men began to run, trying to converge upon the point where those horses threatened to smash a way through the ring of sentries.

Black Hawk steered the horses to a break in the line, dimly seen in the moonlight, and then all in one second it seemed they were through. He had a vision of faces looming out of the darkness, of guns lifting, and he heard the ferocious shouts of an outwitted, thwarted soldiery.

The wildly-charging horses careered into the brush beyond the sentries. Black Hawk risked bullets, and swiftly climbed on to the sweat-slippery, broad back of one of the leading beasts, and balanced there for a second and then leapt wildly into the darkness. He wasn't going to stay on those terrified horses because he knew that very quickly they must run into something and have a stop put to their perilous flight.

As he hit the ground and started to roll he had a momentary impression of the gun carriage and limber seeming to bounce as if on springs high into the air and come turning and twisting down towards him. It had in the end been overturned.

He slithered away like lightning, and those rolling, spinning wheels missed him by a couple of feet. Then there was a crash as the carriage broke up, and the traces became wrapped round a tree and the horses were thrown on to their knees by the sudden cessation of their flight.

When a hundred angry soldiers came rushing up from the camp they found a ruined gun and four terrified but immobile horses in an almost inextricable confusion.

But there was no Black Hawk to be seen.

Black Hawk was walking quietly and without undue haste away from the red glare of the American army camp. He knew there was no need for reckless flight, that he was safe from observation, and to hurry was only to get himself into unnecessary danger.

He walked until he came to a place where the ground became more and more uncertain under his tread, and then he knew that he had come to the mighty swamplands – the Everglades, as the white people called these eerie, treacherous marshlands. Then, because there was no need for further haste, and because he would for certain meet his death in the swamps in the darkness, he lay down and looked at the night sky and then closed his eyes and went to sleep.

He was away at the first hint of light in the morning, and within half an hour he had found the tracks of his people, and was following hard upon them. He found that they had kept to a ridge of high ground which ran like a road through the stinking marshes, and he followed it, and he knew he was gaining upon his people.

A steam rose from the shallow lakes and channels through which he walked, and it drifted between the trees and shortened a man's eyesight, and it made him think that there was movement where there was not.

But Black Hawk, though he had never been in country like this, was a wily hunter, and his quick eyes protected him. It was not of reptiles and birds and beasts that he was afraid; what he feared were the evil spirits which seemed to lurk with the wraith-like spiralling clouds of steam that hung over the avenues between the belts of mangroves. By mid-afternoon he was closing in on his people, he knew. But there were things that Black Hawk didn't know.

And one of those things was that the ridge of high land which his people followed was a road along which other men might walk, and with them horses drawing heavy guns. He didn't know that even then General Jackson was miles back behind him but following this pathway through the swamp-lands.

And what Black Hawk also didn't know was that this was the route to the Spanish fortress on the coast.

4

THE WHITE RIDER

Black Hawk loped tirelessly along that raised causeway which was like a natural road through those
swamp lands. The pangs of hunger were fiercely
ravenous within him, but there was no food, and he
had no time in any event to look for any. The one
urgent thought in his mind was that he must catch
up with his people, and that quickly.

By mid-afternoon a new worry began to come to
the big young Indian, striding along naked save for
that breach clout. He found a tall straight tree that
grew out of the causeway, and he climbed it, in the
hope of seeing his people ahead. But when he was in
the heights of that tall, slender tree, his brown eyes
widened with shock.

He found himself looking straight at the white
'dobe walls of that Spanish fortress.

He looked for his people, frantically, but they were

not anywhere to be seen in the trees which inter-
vened between himself and that fortress built on the
plains that ran by the edge of the sea. His eyes
narrowed against the bright sparkling light from the
distant blue waters, and he stayed there for a long
time, but never once saw movement.

When he descended it was to resume his journey
at an increased speed. It was ominous to him, the fact
that his people had walked straight towards that
fortress instead of taking to one of the side causeways
which struck off occasionally east and west through
the swamps.

As he trotted now, he brooded and he thought. 'If
I had been in charge of that party, I would have gone
to my right in order not to get too close to the white
man's fortress.'

Instinct told Black Hawk that here was treachery.
He knew it at once, and he knew it because he did
not trust the man in charge of that party – Forked
Tongue. He lost much of his caution in order to
make all possible speed and catch up with his
people before they ventured too near the Spanish
garrison.

For the Spaniards were if anything more brutal
than these American soldiers who had driven them
from their lands in Georgia and Tennessee.

It was late in the afternoon when finally he came
out of the swamplands and breathed the fresh exhil-
arating air that blew north from the distant sea. And
still there was no sign of his people. He began to

traverse the bushy plain, so like the prairie where he had spent his youth.

And then he saw a movement ahead of him, and it was so furtive that it sent him down into cover immediately.

Black Hawk remembered then, if he had ever forgotten it, that he was without arms. He was in a territory which could be considered hostile to any Indian, and even many of the Indians who lived on the fringe of the swamp might be enemies. For, silver dollars and white man's whiskey had bought the souls of many a free Indian.

But into Black Hawk's mind came the thought. 'If this isn't a friend I could do with his weapons.' And he went forward on his stomach, using all the guile of woodcraft he had ever known in an effort to come up behind and attack that lurker before he had a chance to use his weapons against the Cherokee brave.

Black Hawk lowered himself cautiously into a dried rain gully which ran across this lumpy, bush-covered plain. He made swift progress, and then he listened, and his ears detected the sound of movement away to his left. Swiftly he came out of that gully and began to glide through the low, stunted bushes that grew less than waist high.

Someone was crouching behind a prickly thorn bush only a few yards from him. Black Hawk froze in his tracks, because it was just possible he had been seen.

Time passed. There was no further movement from beyond that bush, so at length Black Hawk went down on his face again and begun to worm his way around the thorn bush in an effort to get within striking distance of whoever lurked there.

Suddenly he saw something brown, and it was moving, and he realized that whoever lay close up against that bush was turning, and he would be seen.

He had no time for further stalking, but had to risk all in a quick stabbing jump forward, in order to get his hands on his adversary before a weapon could be used against the unarmed warrior.

He was lurching to his feet, flying through the air in one desperate, convulsive movement, his hands reaching forward to grip and hold and immobilise a potentially dangerous opponent.

But even as he came through the air, his hands fell a little, and the strength went out of them. For he saw a face that he recognized – a face that turned at his swift movement and saw him and was filled with fear.

Black Hawk was unable to arrest the forward motion of his attack and he crashed on to that startled, rising form, and they fell together in the dust.

Black Hawk rolled, though, so that his weight did not fall upon the smaller, buckskin-clad person. And when his fall was at an end, he rolled on to his back and looked through the little cloud of rising dust. He was holding at arms-length – lovely Lone Fern.

She looked down at him, and the fear fled from that lovely face and a joyous smile of recognition lit

45

up her countenance. He struggled and sat upright, and she lay against his bent knee, and she was holding his arms just above the elbow in a grip that almost hurt.

Black Hawk said, 'It is good to see you, Lone Fern,'

And Lone Fern answered gravely, saying, 'It is good to see you, Black Hawk.' And then, because she was only a girl and without the stern warrior training that had made Black Hawk the man he was, a sob came to her throat, and she threw herself against the muscular chest of this mighty bronzed warrior.

She forgot she was an Indian. She only knew that she had been terrified, alone there, with heaven knew what number of enemies lurking around her.

She gripped Black Hawk as if she couldn't bear to let him go, now that she had found him again, and Black Hawk put his arms around her and held her and thought that very soon now he would speak what was in his mind – that above all girls he wanted Lone Fern to be his mate.

Then he looked at the sun, which soon would plunge into the distant western sea, and he felt the urgency again within him, and he said, 'Tell me, O Lone Fern, what brings you alone in my path?'

It was a short story, and it was one of suspicion that there was treachery afoot. They had hurried all that day with but little food among them, striking straight south, although in time the wounded among them protested and said that that way led only to the Spanish fortress. And then Forked Tongue had spoken, and she – Lone Fern – had mistrusted his glib statements from the start.

Black Hawk growled, 'He is a man I trust not at any time.'

Forked Tongue had said, 'We are hungry. Maybe there is no food for us even when we get out of this swamp. For our friends the Creeks and Seminoles are a day's march westward from us, and we cannot live that long without food.'

This was true enough, for the children were complaining and the women who dragged them along or carried them in the shawls on their backs were at the end of their strength because they had not eaten for a whole day.

So Forked Tongue said, 'There is food in plenty at the Spanish fortress. They will feed us when I tell them what I know. For do we not know that the American has invaded Spanish territory, and might even now be marching on to this fortress? For this information that danger is approaching, they will assuredly give us the food we need that will take us westward to our friends the Creeks and Seminoles.'

They had received this reasoning uneasily, because no white man was trusted at all. And yet they were in a desperate situation, for there was little chance of finding game so near to a white man's habitation. The white man's guns always drove the game deeper into the wilderness. In the end hunger influenced their decision.

'They decided they would go to the fortress, and

throw themselves upon the mercy of the Spaniard,' said Lone Fern. 'Forked Tongue speaks persuasively, and in time they all began to believe in what he said. And so they went off.'

He released her and held her at arm's length and looked into her face, and he said gently, 'But you did not go with them, O Lone Fern. Why?'

Her eyes brooded into the distance, where the ramparts of that thick-walled fortress lifted above the green of the plain's vegetation. She said: 'It was in my heart that Forked Tongue was not to be trusted. I felt that I would rather die here in the wilderness than in the dungeons of the cruel white invader. I thought I would stay where I could watch that pathway through the swamps, in the hope that some man among our warriors would have survived yesterday's fighting and I would see him as he came through the swamps.'

She didn't say that she had sat there and hoped that if that man wasn't her father, Chief Red Wolf, she wanted it to be this warrior, Black Hawk. Her eyes dropped shyly so that he could not read her thoughts. For if the declaration had to come it should come from the man and not from the maiden she knew.

She had seen a movement as some man came loping out from the swamps, but immediately he had seemed to disappear, and she had sat where she was because it might have been an enemy as much to be feared as the Spaniard behind her.

Big Black Hawk turned again to look at that

48

fortress, white with the long rays of the setting sun reflecting from it. There were palm trees about it and it looked peaceful, but in his heart he shared the mistrust of Lone Fern. He felt that Forked Tongue had more in his mind than he had spoken of to his brethren. He had a feeling that Forked Tongue had some plan for his own salvation, should there be danger lurking at the Spanish fortress for the people he was boldly leading there.

And then the pangs of hunger brought his thoughts away from speculation. He said, 'You are hungry, Lone Fern?'

She nodded and sighed. He spread his empty hands and said, 'I am without weapons even if we do see game. And yet we must eat.'

The situation was desperate enough, and his eyes flickered from place to place, hoping against hope to see game which could be run down by the speed of his legs. Yet he knew it to be hopeless. Without weapons they would starve, here on the broad plains.

He began to strike out westwards, to where the war parties were grouped, as Chief Red Wolf had been told. He took the girl by her hand and they walked together, and in spite of their hunger there was a great content upon them.

And then, an hour or less before dark, a miracle happened.

Right ahead, tantalisingly within bowshot of them, a young deer walked into view from among the thick-growing bushes.

But they were without bow and arrow.

Black Hawk stopped and his hands clenched impotently. For there was food and they were hungry and it could save their lives. Then his fingers opened as if to reach out and grab that plump, fleshy deer, and in his despair he groaned.

Even as he groaned they saw that deer leap high into the air and then crash down, and they knew even as it fell that it was dead.

They stood where they were, watching that still form. For the sharp bark of a rifle had come floating to their ears, and they knew that the prize was not for them but for a man with a gun which could kill Indians equally as well as deer.

It was a white man's gun, they knew instinctively.

Then a man came riding out from among some trees to their left. They went down in a crouch among the bushes, and yet they were able to see him because he rode so high above the level of the vegetation.

And Lone Fern clung suddenly to Black Hawk, for that white man was not riding towards the deer he had killed but straight towards them.

Black Hawk flung Lone Fern to one side and rose to his feet, his eyes flashing fire. He knew then that he had been seen. And Black Hawk was determined to sell his life as dearly as possible, though there was little chance of fighting a man armed with a rifle.

The rider came right up to where Black Hawk stood. And his gun was covering the Indian.

The rider's gun motioned towards where Lone Fern crouched among the bushes. She had been seen, too.

She came out, then, and stood by the side of Black Hawk, and the two faced that white rider. His gun never moved from them as he dismounted.

5

LONE FERN SCREAMED!

The sun's slanting red rays fell full upon the white hunter. For Black Hawk knew at once that that was his calling.

The Indian saw a tall, spare man, with a face browned by sun and wind and exposure to all weathers. He saw blue eyes that looked level and honest and yet now they were shadowed with suspicion.

He wore the buckskin shirt and trousers of the frontier, with a faded blue neck-cloth under a chin that was firm and jutting. On his head was an old hat, but one good enough to shield the eyes from all but a setting sun, and thick enough to turn any rain.

Around his waist was a cartridge belt, and there was a holster slapping on his thigh, in which was a gun – no doubt a six-shooter.

That wasn't altogether usual with a hunter, who relied more upon his rifle than upon a short-range Colt. It augured that this man was a lone wolf, in a land where every man might be his enemy.

They looked at each other, and for a few seconds no one spoke. And then that hunter must have noticed Black Hawk's empty hands, for his gun-barrel began to drop slowly, as if he were relaxing his vigilance a little.

But Black Hawk wasn't deceived. He knew that if he took the slightest step forward, that gun would be up in an instant and pointing at his heart.

Lone Fern came close to the side of her companion. She was frightened of this white man, because in these past weeks every white man they had met had been a cruel and blood-thirsty enemy.

And there was hatred in her brown, blazing eyes, because it was in her heart that that day her father, who was her god, had died under the white man's bullets.

That buckskin-clad hunter suddenly jerked his head, and then indicated with the rifle towards the fallen deer. Black Hawk began to walk to where the beast lay on its side, the flies not yet gathering where blood oozed from a hole neatly put between its eyes. Lone Fern came close behind him.

When they were standing about the beast, that hunter following hard upon their heels and leading his horse, they stood again and looked at each other. And then that white man spoke.

His voice lacked the nasal quality which told of an American. And yet his voice was strong and incisive and spoke the same language.

He said: 'Now, what do I do next?'

He must have read in the Indians' faces the hunger that gripped them, for suddenly he said:

'You hungry?'

Black Hawk didn't speak; didn't indicate those awful pains that gripped him. He stared sombrely into space. He would not exchange words with the white man who spoke from behind the barrel of a deadly rifle.

But Lone Fern spoke. She understood the question and said impulsively:

'Yes . . .'

The strange hunter nodded to Black Hawk and said: 'OK, you make a fire and get that meat cooked.'

Black Hawk didn't stir. He wasn't a white man's servant. He wasn't going to cook this white man's food and then be shot out of hand when he had performed a useful task.

The hunter sighed and leaned on his rifle, standing back from the two Indians. There was just a trace of humour in his blue eyes. He said: 'You don't need to be frightened. I'm no American. I'm – British!'

That brought the Indian's eyes upon him. British! The British more often than not were at war with the Spaniard and the American. And the British had a reputation of being perhaps more considerate to the red man than these mixed races who now called themselves an American nation. As for the Spaniards . . .

The Britisher spoke again. 'I'm Jim Tyler, I hunt anything between the Atlantic and Pensacola. I don't have many friends,' he said humorously. 'But I suppose the Indians along the coast plain are more companionable than Americans or Spaniards. So you see, red brother, if you keep your distance you have nothing to fear. We shall eat together.'

Lone Fern seemed to grasp the situation ahead of Black Hawk. She sensed, because she understood less perfectly that alien language, that the hunter meant them no harm, but he was suspicious of their intentions, and did not intend them to get the drop on him.

She turned to Black Hawk and spoke urgently in Cherokee. 'He means well, O Black Hawk. Let us make this fire, because I am hungry and here is food.'

She didn't wait for Black Hawk to change his mind. Instead, she ran to a tree and began to strip away bark which wouldn't smoke and betray their position. She cunningly got a fire going, with the aid of flint and tinder loaned to her in a box by the white hunter, who sat apart and watched them.

He was a very careful man, that lean hunter named Jim Tyler.

Black Hawk turned to the deer. Then he shrugged. He had no knife to cut away the hide of the beast. Tyler divined what was in his mind, and he called:

'Here!' and threw across his keen bladed hunting-knife.

Within minutes the haunches of the deer were on sticks and rotating above the fire. And skewered on long twigs were the tongue and liver and small, juicy morsels of venison. And these Black Hawk and Lone Fern held on either side of the fire and slowly turned them, and the scent of cooking meat came into their nostrils and made them frantic because now there was nothing else they wanted in the world except food.

In time it was cooked – or cooked sufficiently for the needs of the hungry Indians.

But even then Black Hawk could not forget the dignity of his Cherokee upbringing. He walked across to Jim Tyler, a long skewer of meat extended.

Tyler took it nodding his thanks, and Black Hawk went back to the fire to share that other skewer of meat with Lone Fern. When they had finished, there were slices of cooked meat that could be taken from the haunches.

There came a time when they wanted no more, and there was no deer left for them to eat.

They lay down, then, and rested, while Jim Tyler sat and watched them.

His voice broke through the content which followed like a drug upon their meal.

He said: 'I think I met your people yesterday. You are Cherokees, aren't you?' He was thinking of that moment when, out hunting, he had watched the headlong flight of that band of Indians, men, women and children. Of all places, they had come within yards of where he lay hidden, and then settled down to rest.

He spoke little of the Cherokee language, but he had heard enough to understand their plight.

'The damned Yankees have driven you from your lands in Georgia and Tennessee, isn't that right?' To the Britisher it was an old story. The land-hungry emigrants to America would not leave anything to the Indian. Always just when the Indian had settled on new territory, another wave of emigrants came to push them farther west.

Now he knew that the cry was – no more Indians on the east side of the Mississippi! Some day, he thought ironically, the cry would be: 'And no more Indians on the west of the Mississippi, either!'

He hadn't shown himself, though he had no unfriendly feelings towards these northern, prairie Indians. Rather, as a free hunter himself, he could sympathize with them in their plight. But it had been better for him to remain hidden, as he did, because in their harassed, desperate mood, undoubtedly at his appearance the Indian braves would immediately have shot him down.

Black Hawk sat up and looked at him. He was a bold man, and the thought came to him now that as this white hunter seemed not unfriendly, he might be of use to him and Lone Fern.

He said: 'Did you see any others of my tribe, this side of the swamplands?'

Jim Tyler shook his head. His horse was cropping behind him, and there was that rifle still lying across his knees. Jim Tyler wasn't the kind of man to be surprised by anyone in the bush or by this Indian whom he had just fed.

Black Hawk did not attempt to come closer recognizing that there was a limit to the friendliness which this hunter dared show him. He asked, though: 'Have you been to the Spanish fortress today?'

Jim Tyler shook his head. There was no reason for him to keep away from the Spanish fortress, as the Spaniards were more friendly with Britishers than with the strident, avaricious Americans from the far north. But he just didn't like to stay around buildings with a lot of people. He was working his way south to these great plains where there was still an abundance of game and he had purposely avoided the post.

His answer disappointed Black Hawk.

He wanted news of his people and he suspected that if they had been led into the Spanish post, they would now be in some peril or other.

Something in the Indian's manner aroused the curiosity of the lean hunter. Perhaps the worry and disappointment on the Indian's face was plain to his sharp eyes and he was intrigued by it.

He said: 'What's worrying you?'

There was something in the way he said those three words that seemed to strike a chord in Black

Hawk's heart. At once he knew that, for all his attitude of guarded suspicion, this big Britisher was
friendly towards the red man. So he told him of his
worries.

He told him of Forked Tongue, a man he did not
trust, and he told how his people – the women and
children and the aged and disabled of their tribe –
had gone with Forked Tongue into the fortress of an
enemy more savage toward the red man than the
Americans from whom they were fleeing.

True, sometimes for their own purposes the
Spaniards used the Indians. But Black Hawk said that
it was in his heart that this was not one of those times.

He rose to his feet and looked eastwards to where
the fortress was a tiny patch of white in the rays of the
dying sun. Inside, he thought, were his people – the
people they had fought for and in so many cases
given their lives to protect.

He was thinking that in the end it had turned out
to be a waste of effort. Because he had no doubt
himself that inside that fortress there would be no
sanctuary for the red man.

Jim Tyler put out a corn cob which he had been
smoking. His voice was grim when he spoke, and
evidently he shared Black Hawk's suspicions. 'Those
Spaniards are capable of anything if they are that way
inclined.' His eyes turned and looked towards that
post, too.

He stood and brooded there for a time, his heart
heavy. And now there was no suspicion between

Indian and Britisher. Now they stood together in amity.

Suddenly that curious Britisher said, 'I'm going to that fortress. I'm going to see what those Spaniards intend to do with your people.' His voice rose to anger. 'I won't stand by and see helpless men and women and children put to the sword as these Spaniards have done before!'

They heard him with their hearts leaping, and a sense of rising excitement inside them. Lone Fern was thinking, 'The Great Spirit has found us this friend. He is a man among white men!'

They saw him mount, and the shadows of evening were upon him. He looked round him to get his bearings, so that he would remember this place, and then he called down to them, 'You wait here and I'll be back by sunrise to tell you what's happening at the post.'

But he didn't say what they could do if they found that their worst suspicions were correct – that in fact a deadly fate had been apportioned as the lot of those weary, homeless Indians.

They saw him ride eastwards to where the white Spanish fortress gleamed in the last rays of the sun. It was but a few hours' ride for a man mounted on a good horse, and they knew that he would find his way to the post in the moonlight without difficulty.

They went back to the fire, and now there was a gladness in their hearts, and when they looked at each other they were almost smiling. For now they could rest their weary limbs and leave it to this friendly white man to learn what awaited their kind.

Lone Fern went and stretched herself alongside a thorn bush which would give cover to the gentle stealing wind they could expect after dark. Black Hawk heard her murmur, 'A few white men are good.'

He said nothing. After this day when his life had nearly been taken by white men, and when so many of his tribe had died before the fury of the palefaces' guns, he had no heart to say anything good about the invaders.

He made Lone Fern rise, though, and he took her to where a stunted tree upreared among the bushes. He lifted her into its branches, and she understood. Here she would be hidden from the view of night marauders.

But there was no room for Black Hawk in the tree, and he went and stretched himself some yards away, where he could keep his ear to the ground even as he slept. She fixed herself comfortably between two crooked branches, and then her heavy eyes closed and she fell asleep.

When she awoke it was to see a sight that brought a betraying scream to her lips . . . .

It was less than two hours later that Black Hawk came to instant wakefulness. Something had stirred. Somewhere close at hand there had been movement, and movement of any kind was hostile to them right then.

Black Hawk came swiftly on to his knees, his hand grasping the thick club that he had fashioned and hardened at the fire earlier in the evening. His eyes strained into the darkness.

Minutes flitted by with only a faint moonlight playing between the rounded bushes which looked so much like crouching forms.

He turned silently, and without moving surveyed every point around him. And then he heard that movement again, and now his eyes riveted upon the place where he had heard it.

In time he saw a movement of a bush when there was no wind blowing, and he knew that an enemy lurked behind it. After some minutes he caught another movement and realized that someone was approaching their fire.

That fire had been put out right after their meal, but it is the way of wood smoke to hang in the air, and keen-nosed men could detect it a mile away and using their nostrils like a dog's they could come against the wind and trace it.

Someone was creeping slowly forward, intent upon discovering who had made this fire.

Black Hawk saw a slight movement on the edge of the clearing, only thirty yards or so away from him. And it was right beneath the tree where Lone Fern slept.

His heart beat violently. He thought, 'Perhaps they will hear her as she breathes in her sleep.'

He crouched now, tensed and ready to spring to

her rescue if she were detected and attacked.

A shadowy form came flittering soundlessly across from the bushes where the blackened heap of ashes threw out a pungent aroma.

And then Black Hawk saw another figure flit from the darkness and come and join that first one, and behind the second man was a third . . . a fourth . . . and others. . . .

They were between him and Lone Fern, and they were settling by that fire in the manner of men who had no intention of leaving yet awhile.

The veins stood out on Black Hawk's forehead with the intensity of his passion, and the club shook in his hand because of the emotion which gripped him.

If they were to remain at this burnt-out fire all night then for certain he and Lone Fern would be detected when dawn came. Despairingly he thought, 'Once again we are trapped!'

A shadowy, shambling figure suddenly rose in the darkness behind Black Hawk. Because of his frantic concern over Lone Fern, Black Hawk had been unwary and had failed to see yet another man creeping towards the fire from behind.

Black Hawk went rolling out into the moonlight of that tiny glade, where the men were tearing at the skin and bones and all that was left of the deer.

It was at that moment that Lone Fern looked down and saw the silent struggle in the moonlight, and then she screamed before she had time to check the sound which rose involuntarily to her lips.

But at that moment Black Hawk was rolling from underneath that shambling adversary, and the moon fell upon that face, and then Black Hawk received yet another shock . . . .

6

IN THE FORTRESS

Jim Tyler rode eastwards as hard as he could go while the light lasted. As he rode his lips were compressed in a thin, hard line.

He was a curious man, this Jim Tyler – a man certainly out of the ordinary. For he was more than a hunter – he was a British secret agent, unpaid and unrecognized, but loyal to his country's interests and always sending reports when matters seemed to concern his native land.

For some time now his people in faraway London, England, had been uneasy about the rise to power of the new American nation. Especially they viewed with doubt America's obvious attempts to bring Spanish-dominated Texas, California and Florida within the United States.

Now it seemed their doubts were crystallized. A headstrong American general, without any authority from Congress, had taken it upon himself to invade Florida with the intention of wresting it by force from the lethargic Spaniard. Following a defeated tribe of hapless Indians had only been an excuse to cross the border, Tyler could see.

He wanted to hurry off to get a message through to his people about this Florida incident, because control of Florida by the Americans might become a threat to Britain's possessions in the West Indies.

But he found he couldn't just ride away and leave helpless Indians to a sorry fate. He was a man who had lived among Indians and counted many as his friends. He hated to see the way they were knocked about, and found himself constantly championing their cause.

No, he thought, time wasn't so urgent that he couldn't go out of his way to try to help the Cherokees.

After all, he owed his information to those two Cherokees – that fine young warrior, and that gracious, lovely, Indian maiden.

He thought back to the shooting of that deer. He'd been lying across a deer trail, waiting patiently for his supper to come into view. He'd seen the deer and sighted and fired all in one movement – and right in the act of firing he had caught a movement out of the corner of his eye . . . had turned and seen these two Indians. He'd gone across to them imme- diately, wary, but ready to be friends . . .

It was dark when finally Jim Tyler came riding across the plain to within sight of the lights in the harbour and from the town grouped around it. When he was within sound of the surf breaking on the shore, he halted in a thick brake and dismounted.

Once before he had passed through this country, and he knew the topography of this fortress called Santa Maria. There was a good, deep harbour at this point, and the Spaniards had built a high, thick, stone wall across the harbour end of the creek. Within were grouped the houses of those Indians who served their Spanish masters, some negroes and a few Spanish traders and craftsmen. To the north of the creek, close against the high wall, reared the 'dobe fortress itself.

Jim remembered it for a very solid affair, though it was neglected, as were all Spanish possessions in the Americas. The Spanish were too indolent, and allowed decay and rot to set in, and because of that they were gradually being pushed out of the North American continent by the more Nordic immigrants.

Now he saw light reflecting on water, and the dark silhouettes of tapering masts against a moonlight sky. He saw feathered palm trees as a background to the looming shadowy mass of the fortress itself.

He left his horse where it was, and moved forward on foot. He knew where he was going and what he was going to do.

He came to the high, solid, wooden gate that was set into the massive fortress wall, and he kicked upon it with his boots.

That in itself proved the indolence of these Spanish soldiers. If they had been alert and at their posts he would have been challenged long before he reached the big gate.

A sleepy, surly voice shouted down to him from an embrasure above. The language was Spanish.

'Who's there? Who comes at this tune of night?'

'Señor, it is a traveller who has had to leave his horse and finish his journey on foot,' called Jim Tyler in the same language. This was true enough, and no lie, although undoubtedly that Spanish sentry obtained a wrong inference.

There was a lot of grumbling within, but then the gate commander finally relented and came and opened a small wicket gate set in the main one, and invited Tyler to step through it.

The British secret agent came through and found himself at once the object of a close, suspicious scrutiny in the light of a lamp held to inspect him.

He saw three or four lamplit faces, chiefly remarkable for their gauntness, and their unshaven appearance. For soldiers they were a disgrace, and Jim Tyler had contempt in his eyes as he looked at them.

He knew there was disease around this coast which sapped the strength of men, but he knew there was no excuse for this unmilitary appearance of the Spanish soldiers.

He asked for a night's lodging. He could pay well for it, he said, tapping his pocket.

The guard commander looked at him and said,

not altogether unpleasantly, 'The commandant will see you first, Señor.'

Evidently the commandant saw everyone who arrived at Fort Santa Maria, and the lateness of the hour made no exception.

In fact, the commandant was not yet in bed, but was sitting on a balcony overlooking the sparkling moonlit bay a drink in a slender glass in his hand. Tyler was escorted to his presence, passing through the fortress to do so.

It should have been a gracious place that fortress, for all its military significance; but everywhere there was dirt and disorder, and the walls were crumbling and there was a need for paint and whitewash that would have made it more healthy and cooler. Even so there was a pleasantness about the Moorish arches and the wide, lofty rooms through which Tyler was led. And that balcony was a place for relaxation, enough to satisfy any man with its superb view.

Only Tyler wasn't there to admire scenery. He was using his eyes all the time, remembering the way he was led in, and looking for evidence of Indian prisoners. For he felt certain they would now be prisoners.

The commandant was a lean, sallow grandee. He had a small, pointed, aristocratic beard, and a tiny spiky moustache.

Tyler, looking down at him from between two guards, thought that if the commandant had had the jacket cleaned more often, and the gold lacings sewn where they had become detached from the tunic material, he would have looked more impressive.

As it was that commandant did not look the kind of man anyone would want for a friend.

Tyler thought, 'This man can be cruel.' For there was about the Spaniard's eyes a latent hint of viciousness. When his eyes looked at Tyler they were insolent, aggressive, as if inviting him to some sort of verbal combat.

Tyler thought grimly, 'Yes, he's the kind to enjoy trouble when he's in his own fortress and surrounded by supporters.' But he wouldn't have been quite the same where conditions were more equal, the Britisher thought.

The commandant questioned Tyler in an aggressive tone. Why was he out so late at night?

Tyler repeated his story to the sentry, and it seemed satisfactory.

What nationality was he? British? What was a Britisher doing in Spanish territory?

Tyler merely said that he was a hunter and was working his way across into Texas. He looked at the commandant challengingly, and said: 'Our countries are not at war. Why should I not ride through Spanish territory?'

The commandant didn't like being spoken to in this way, and told him to shut up. Plainly he was in the mood to deal roughly with people who earned his displeasure.

And then the commandant leaned forward, his

sharp brown eyes watching the Britisher's face.

'There's a story that Americans have ridden into Florida. This was told to me by Indians who said they had suffered in battle on Spanish territory across the great swamps. What do you know about that?' the commandant rapped.

Tyler shrugged. He said, 'I saw Cherokee Indians on the run from American soldiers. But I rode away, and if there was a battle, I didn't see it'

He knew from what Black Hawk and Lone Fern had told him that there had been a battle, but he was not anxious to give this insolent commandant any more information than he need. Let the fellow find out things for himself, he thought angrily.

And then he received a mild shock. For the commandant looked at him and said coolly. 'You are a spy of the Americanos.'

Tyler shook his head wearily. These Spanish people were always looking for spies. If only they would look for a bit of work instead, they would have a more healthy community, he thought.

The commandant was suddenly tired. He wanted to contemplate the night sky and get himself drunk so that he would sleep late in bed next morning and thus miss part of another weary, intolerable day when nothing happened.

Abruptly he ordered Tyler to be taken and kept under guard for the night. The two guards marched Jim away and took him down to the guard-room beneath the gate.

71

This was upsetting to Tyler, who had wanted freedom within the fortress walls in order to be able to look for the Cherokees. So he viewed with concern his incarceration in the guard-room.

He needn't have worried!

The guards were as annoyed at receiving him as he was at sharing their bug-infested quarters.

The guard commander gave his opinion, rapidly, volubly, and at great length. The brown eyes flashed anger at this man who threatened to disturb his peace.

In the end everybody did just what they had been doing before – they did what they would have done if they had had no prisoner in their midst.

Tyler was made to occupy a bed at the rear of the guard-room. His arms had been taken from him and were stacked carelessly in a corner by the door. The guard commander settled himself down to sleep, instructing the other guards to keep awake and watch their prisoner.

When the guard commander was asleep the two remaining guards within the guard-room tossed for it and one won and promptly stretched himself and went to sleep.

The loser looked sourly at the snoring sleepers, and then stretched himself and made himself as comfortable as possible where he could watch their prisoner.

In ten minutes he was fast asleep, too. Jim Tyler shook his head in disgust. These Spanish soldiers were the worst in the world. How they had come to conquer most of known America, he couldn't understand.

He simply walked out of that guardroom, collecting his guns as he came by the door. He wasn't in a hurry, either, for looking back at that trio of snoring men he knew they wouldn't waken for hours.

He passed out into the plaza, that open square between the fortress wall and the main block of the fortress itself.

Tyler moved swiftly, once he was in the moonlit plaza. Though he felt sure that his 'guards' were capable of sleeping soundly until the dawn, he could not ignore the possibility of their being wakened by something.

As he crept into the long, deep shadows where the main entrance to the fort was, he wondered how good his luck would be. If guards were due to be relieved shortly, he would find himself in a tight fix. On the other hand, it was quite likely that he would have half an hour or an hour or more, and that should be sufficient for his mission.

The big, iron-studded main doorway into the fort was open to let a cooling draught of air pervade the building.

He went inside. Moonlight was the only illumination within the building just then. It came through the long, church-like windows, and reflected from a tiled floorway within the main hall.

He crouched, watchful, his eyes on those rounded

Moorish arches, so deep in shadow that they could have contained a hundred enemies. He was about to mount the broad, stone stairway that led up to the commandant's quarters, his idea being to find a position high up where he could look down over the small town within the wall, when he heard footsteps approaching.

He heard the sound of men climbing steps, and they came slowly and with labour as if they had been climbing a long time.

Tyler listened, and realized that the footsteps were approaching a massive door set into one of the shadowy archways right across from him. He shrank back into the gloom, and his eyes riveted on that doorway.

He heard the jangling of keys, and then the crash of belts, and then men came stepping out as the door swung ponderously open.

There were three of them. Two were in the bedraggled uniform of Spanish soldiery. They carried rifles, but they carried them carelessly, and it would have taken little to have surprised them.

The third man walked between them, and he was naked save for a breech clout.

He was an Indian, a Cherokee, Jim Tyler thought at once.

He looked at that black glossy hair with its horned head-dress, and then looked upon a broad dark face with a curiously wide, thin mouth.

For some reason almost immediately the thought came to Tyler, 'This is Forked Tongue!'

He had nothing to go on, but the hunch remained. He saw one of the guards slam the door and lock it from the outside and shoot back corresponding bolts on this side of the unpainted door. Then one of the guards said something quickly in Spanish and jerked his head towards the stairs, and all three began to mount.

Tyler glided after them. His moccasins making no sound, the buck-skin clad British secret-agent kept to the shadows of the winding staircase, following by sound now and not by sight in case the soldiers ahead turned and saw him.

They passed along a familiar corridor, and then one of the guards stopped outside a door and tapped on it, and at once the imperative voice of the grandee fort commander gave a peremptory 'Enter!' to the men.

The trio marched through the doorway, and then the door came to.

Tyler looked around, but though there was sound of stirrings down the passage, he saw no one and he risked a quick glide forward towards that door.

He heard voices within, but to his disappointment he couldn't hear what was being said.

Taking a risk, he gently opened the door. The voices were plainer to his ears now.

It seemed that the commandant was questioning the Indian anew. Where exactly had these American forces been? he wanted to know. Were they close up to the great swamp, or many miles north of it?

The Indian replied in a mixture of Spanish, English and his own language, so that it was difficult to understand what he was saying.

It seemed to Tyler, though, that the commandant in the end was satisfied that in fact American troops were on Spanish soil. It seemed to cause him little concern, however. Indeed, once he said comfortably, 'They are far away. Perhaps they will not come through those stinking swamps.'

He didn't want to stir his idle thoughts and begin preparations for a defence in case an army did appear against the fortress. Mañana, was his attitude. Tomorrow . . .

But then the conversation changed. Now that Indian was speaking more fluently, and there was a persuasiveness about his tongue.

Tyler heard him make an infamous proposition to that fort commandant.

'We are your prisoners, O Great One,' the Indian said fawningly. 'I do not know what is in your mind for me and my people—'

The fort commandant lit a long black cheroot, and blew smoke and interrupted him with, 'Your people are good for nothing but the plantations in Cuba.' His tone was unpleasant and arrogant. 'They will be put aboard a French corsair when it arrives in a few days' time, and will be taken where their American enemies cannot do them any harm.'

He seemed to find a little humour in his state-ment, and he laughed unpleasantly, and his glittering eyes surveyed that Indian standing before him.

Forked Tongue – if it was he – met that gaze with eyes just as glittering and bright. There was a calculating look on his face as he said, 'We came to you in hunger, O Great One. We did not expect to be taken prisoners and made slaves.'

The Spanish commandant was disposed to be facetious about it. 'It is not what dogs like you expect. It is for great ones like myself to decide upon the future of people like you.'

'But,' said, that Indian cunningly, 'I am too valuable to you merely to be sold into slavery.'

They looked at each other. They were birds of a feather, both steeped in treachery, and perhaps both recognizing it. But the Spanish grandee merely said coldly, 'I have enough Indian servants about the fortress. Many more might become dangerous.'

Forked Tongue seemed to move a little nearer to where the commandant lounged in that plaited, basket Indian chair. His voice dropped a little, and his tone became eager. 'But perhaps I could be the means of bringing many more Indians for your slaves!' he said eagerly.

The commandant removed his cheroot at that and looked with some interest at the Indian now. He didn't speak, and so Forked Tongue became emboldened and spoke again.

'There will be other Indians in the country,' he said quickly. 'I know where there are Creeks and Seminoles, and I could pursuade some of them, in little parties, to come to you – perhaps by telling them that you were harbouring wounded Cherokees who needed assistance into Indian country.'

The Spaniard was beginning to catch on, and he had removed his feet from a small stool and was sitting forward, his eyes upon that treacherous Indian.

'Your plan has some merit,' the Spaniard said slowly, his eyes never leaving that brown, broad face before him. 'But what guarantee have I that if I let you go you will ever return to keep your promise to me?'

Forked Tongue shrugged quickly, almost contemptuously. 'I am a man who desires wealth,' he said brusquely. 'I want money so that I can go and live in the northern States, where Indians live alongside white men and no harm comes to them. I am tired of this southern country where always we are at war with white men.'

'You want money, eh?'

'I want money. I want the silver dollars of the Americans in such number that I shall not want if I go north to live in their cities.'

Standing beside that partly-opened door Tyler's eyes grew grim and hard as he heard the callous statements of this Indian who would buy his own life and comfort by delivering into the hands of their enemies his own people.

He thought he heard a sound along the passage-way, but when he looked no one was there, and he thought it was probably a rat. There were plenty of rats within this fortress, he thought, and one of them was the Indian who propounded this bargain to the Spaniard!

'Give me ten silver dollars for every Creek and Seminole I deliver into your hands,' said Forked Tongue. 'You can get more than ten dollars from a slaver, and both of us will be satisfied.'

The long sallow face of that bearded grandee commandant nodded slowly, as if satisfied with what he saw and heard. His manner seemed to say. 'I have judged you well. You will not betray me. Your desire for silver is strong upon you, and you will do as you say.'

He was saying, 'You shall be released with the first light of dawn. You will be paid, as you wish – that is, ten dollars for every Indian you deliver into my hands.'

The commandant even looked pleased wth himself, because he could see in this treacherous Indian a chance to earn himself many slavers' dollars. And at the back of his cunning mind was the thought. 'When you have done, you, too, will go into a slave ship hold!'

Jim Tyler heard that sound again, and this time he knew it was no rat. He wheeled. Tip-toeing down the passage towards him were three partly-dressed Spaniards. They had guns in their hands, and these were not carelessly held, but were pointing at the buckskin-clad Britisher.

He had a glimpse of sallow faces, unshaven and unprepossessing. He saw hard, suspicious eyes upon him, and he knew that in being found where he was, he had forfeited all right to mercy.

He threw himself sideways, and immediately those guns blazed off towards him.

7

THE TRAP!

As he crashed on to the broad floor of the landing, he fired. His bullet went closely over the heads of those three startled Spaniards. The crashing roar of his rifle mingled with the duller, heavier boom of their more antiquated weapons.

Tyler heard lead scream past his head as he went down on to the floor, and plaster showered from the walls around him. He fell down those steps, so frantic were his movements in order to get round the corner out of sight of his three enemies.

The place was in an uproar. Everywhere men were shouting, and the hullabaloo had already spread to the wall outside. His escape from the guard-room would now be discovered.

Tyler picked himself up off those stairs and went bounding down as fast as his legs could take him. He didn't want to be caught inside this fortress. There might never be any coming out for him afterwards if he did.

For now that commandant could have him shot for being a spy within a military precinct.

He got down into the main hall and raced towards the big door. Suddenly he saw someone loom up out of the darkness, as if racing to enter the building. He swung his rifle and the butt came over, and though the man started to turn, the butt caught him and sent him reeling and shouting in pain against the wall.

Tyler was outside now, under the moonlight. From the guard-room they saw his racing figure flitting from shadow to shadow towards the end of the fortress wall. Recklessly they opened fire. They weren't within yards of their illusive target, so bad was their marksmanship.

But Tyler didn't count upon their bad aim. He leapt forward with greater speed until he had reached the corner of the main block.

He found a cobbled roadway here, which led off the mound on which the fortress was built, down into the town below. He wanted to get through that town and find an unguarded place on the wall which surrounded this harbour, so that he could get over it and reach his horse out on the moonlit plain.

Everywhere men were running and shouting, and torches were blazing as search parties began to look for him in the shadows. As the spreading roar of sound reached this town of 'dobe and reed buildings he heard voices calling out from within, and then people began to appear.

They were men of many nationalities, and they came out with guns ready, not knowing what to expect. When the British hunter and secret agent saw them, he swerved and dodged behind a row of mud houses, until he was right within that little town. Then boldly he went out and joined the disturbed sleepers, and he walked and that was unexpected and nobody looked twice at him in the moonlight.

But the guards were streaming down that cobbled roadway, two or three dozen of them in a line now, with red flaming torches held above their hastily donned peaked guardees' hats.

Tyler knew that once they brought those lights into this town and began a systematic search of the place, he would be discovered.

Suddenly he pointed towards the harbour, and shouted in Spanish. 'There he goes!'

At once an excited throng of civilians and soldiery streamed off to where the dark shapes of vessels lay moored to the stone quayside.

Tyler let them go, and then audaciously began to walk back towards the fortress.

It seemed to him that it would be safer to scale the wall at a point where ladders led up to a cat-walk where the guards patrolled, rather than try to scramble up the wall at a point nearer the harbour where there was no convenient ladder.

He went walking beneath the wall, and his luck was in, for any sentries who were above didn't see him for the shadow, and anyway were intent upon the search that was going on among the shipping in the harbour. Tyler glided along the wall until he came to a ladder that he had noticed up by the gate.

He was about to ascend it, his gun ready for action in case he ran into a sentry on the cat-walk immediately above, when he heard a violent commotion from outside the gate.

He groaned, because in an instant that had alerted the sentries and brought them crowding down to this end where the ladder was. He shrank farther back into the shadow, and awaited developments.

Voices shouted from outside, demanding entry. An exasperated and suspicious guard commander took a lot of precautions before he finally opened the main gate. Half a dozen riders rode into the moonlit plaza.

Tyler caught a glimpse of them, and realized they were Indians – probably Choctaw Indians who had found employment in the Spanish service. They swung off their horses as the fort commandant came striding angrily out from the main block.

Tyler saw that one rider didn't dismount. He was lying across the saddle of his horse, face down in the manner of a man who is tied by hands and feet under the belly of his mount.

And Tyler saw that this man wore a uniform which was probably blue in daylight – he saw by the cut that he was a soldier of the United States' army.

He saw something else, too. He saw a chance of escape!

The guards who should have been closing those two massive gates, were doing it slowly, their attention attracted by the grouped Indians with their prisoner behind them.

Tyler simply walked straight towards the closing gates. They must have seen him approaching, but the fact that he approached upright and at a normal walking pace lulled their sense of danger and they never so much as glanced at him. Far more interesting was this American prisoner who had been brought in by their Indian allies.

When Tyler was a mere yard or so from the ponderously closing gates, one of the guards did shift his eyes, and then they widened incredulously because of what they saw so near to them.

Tyler risked everything in a mighty leap between the gates. He was through and on the outside before a startled yell from the guard brought everyone's eyes round towards the gateway.

But then it was too late. The very weight of those gates kept them moving, even though the guards immediately threw thenselves backwards in an attempt to keep them open. They crashed together, and now six inches of stout wooden planking were between the fleeing Britisher and his enemies.

Jim even found time to chuckle to himself, as he leapt towards the bush-covered plain which represented safety to him. It had all been so easily done, so miraculously simple, that even he couldn't credit his escape.

Then a shot rang out, and he knew that he wasn't free yet. He raced headlong for the looming bushes behind which he would have cover, and all along that high, castellated wall red flames stabbed and broke the darkness. The noise from beyond the wall was frantic now. The fort commandant would be beside himself in rage.

Lead whistled by his ears and even tore at his fringed buckskin sleeve, but with every yard he took he was getting into greater safety, and then finally came a glad moment when he dived behind thick bushes and he knew they could no longer see him.

He went quickly deeper into those bushes, on hands and knees until he knew it was safe for him to stand upright.

And then he began to run again, because he feared that Spanish troops might be sent after him to beat through the bushes and find this resourceful Britisher who had outwitted them.

For a time he had difficulty in locating his whereabouts, but then suddenly he came out among some trees which were familiar and he ran on after that, straight to where his patient horse was waiting for him.

He mounted without hurry. Now those Spaniard wouldn't catch him. He reloaded, and then set his horse to a careful walk eastwards.

Half an hour later he ran into an American scouting party.

All at once he saw flittering forms in the darkness, and instantly he stabbed his heels into his horse's sides and sent it leaping forward.

They must have been just as surprised as he was, and they didn't fire in any event, probably because they didn't wish to alarm the fort.

But Tyler heard startled voices, and saw men reel back as his mighty stallion bounded into top speed instantly.

Those voices were nasal and American, and he knew at once that they were United States' forces – it would be one of these, he guessed, who had been taken prisoner by those Choctaw Indians and carried to their master, the Spanish commandant.

Recklessly he let his horse gallop through the darkness for about fifty yards or so, and then he pulled it down to a walk again. For those men had been afoot, and would not be able to catch up with him, even if they had wanted to, while he was mounted.

He breathed a sigh of relief, because it had been a startling encounter, and one not at all expected. He looked at the stars and wiped his face, because he discovered that the past moments had made him sweat profusely in the warm night air.

And then he struck off westwards, and he rode until he knew he was close upon the place where he had left those two Indians.

He didn't fear treachery from them. Black Hawk

had looked a fine type of warrior, so without undue precaution, he sent his horse slowly forward towards that tiny glade where he had shot the deer.

The moon was full upon him, and he could see his way well. He came out to that glade, and he knew it because his keen nostrils got the smell of lingering wood smoke.

He halted his horse, and peered around him, wondering where his Indian friends were sleeping.

And then someone came up from behind a bush within a few yards of him, and he saw that it was an Indian. And then he saw another movement on the other side and that was an Indian.

And then all at once, everywhere around him, were grey, ghostly forms, and they were all Indians.

And when he looked around at them his eyes failed to see Black Hawk or that lovely Indian maiden who had been with him, Lone Fern.

He started to fling himself from the saddle, his gun leaping forward to fire at his moonlit opponents. But even as he fell, a frantic thought inside him said, 'It is too late! You walked into a trap!'

8

THE KEYS!

Lone Fern's eyes opened upon a scene of struggling forms, there in the moonlight of that tiny glade among the crowding, sinister-grey bushes. She screamed before she knew what she was doing, because it seemed to her that Black Hawk, this warrior she wanted for herself, was being overwhelmed or possibly killed.

But Black Hawk was fighting desperately, because he had seen for one fleeting instant a face – and to him it had seemed that it was the face of a ghost, only ghosts didn't have warm flesh and blood, and this one had.

He was calling, 'Running Elk!' and there was astonishment in his mind that Running Elk should be alive after that battle on the far side of the swamplands.

There was confusion among his attackers then,

and they began to fall away and release him and he was able to sit up and stare round at them.

Lone Fern dropped from the tree and came and ran to his side, because that was where a man's mate should be when he faced danger. Together they looked round at the encircling forms, and then their eyes truly widened and their mouths opened with astonishment.

That was Running Elk, and there was Leaping Wind, and that sturdy form could only be Brown Bear.

In an instant Black Hawk was on his feet, and his friends were crowding round him. They forgot caution for the moment in the delight of their meeting. Black Hawk's voice rang out incredulously 'I thought you were all dead. I thought I was the only one who had survived that battle!'

But his eyes were counting and he saw that around him were at least a dozen of the men who had gone so bravely to do battle against the superior forces of the American army.

The voices spoke back to him, and they were well-remembered voices, and it did his heart good to know that a few others – all too few – had escaped that day with their lives.

Running Elk came and put his hands upon the warrior's shoulders and embraced him, because Black Hawk was a favourite among the leaders of the tribe.

'You are welcome, O Son,' the big, shambling

warrior chief told him. 'We thought you were dead, along with the others, and our hearts grieved for you because Black Hawk is known as the bravest of all the Cherokees, and we still have need of our braves.'

The rapturous greeting died with the realization that though a few had survived, yet most of their kind had perished in the defence of their fleeing women and children and old folk. They sat around the burnt blackness that had been a fire, but they didn't attempt to kindle it again because fire brought enemies through the darkness.

And again they fell upon the bones and flesh that adhered to the skin of that deer – some even chewed on the skin itself. For they had a great hunger upon them, because they had found little to eat in the awful trek through the swamplands.

They had fought until the end had been too obvious and then they had pulled away, the two or three of each group that had survived. But even then they had stayed within distance of their enemies, prepared to resume the fight if they began a pursuit of their people. They had seen cavalry ride out, but quickly return when they had found that their enemies had escaped.

And then the Indians had come together shortly before dusk and begun to follow a trail through the swamplands.

They had not followed by the same route as their womenfolk, but had taken a shorter way, expecting to meet with them as they branched westwards to where the Creek and Seminole camp was expected to be.

But though they had come out of the swamplands before sunset they had not found any tracks leading westward along this great plain, as they had expected. This had worried them and they had begun to move along the coast plain, hoping to join up with their people.

Instead, in the darkness Brown Bear's keen nostrils had detected the scent of wood smoke still hanging among the bushes. They had come forward to investigate, thinking that perhaps some of their tribe might be encamped quite close to them. And then Running Elk, who had more guile than any other man in their tribe, had seen that crouching form in the moonlight and had leapt upon him from behind.

His surprise at seeing Black Hawk had been as great as that warrior's amazement at seeing his old friend again.

Black Hawk sat with them, and Lone Fern was close to his side for she knew now that she was the mate of this bold warrior's choice. She knew it though no word had yet been spoken on the matter between them.

And Black Hawk, with bitterness on his tongue, told of what he knew and of what he surmised.

'Our people went straight along a causeway through the swamplands into the fortress of the Spaniard, who is no better than these Americanos who drove us from our lands.'

At that there was a murmur of surprise, followed

by a rumble of swift, rising anger from the other braves.

There was one who queried quickly, 'Why did they go there? Why did they not avoid the fortress?'

Black Hawk replied as Lone Fern had told him. 'They were near to their end because of lack of food. They were willing to believe anything that Forked Tongue told them. And when he said they would be welcomed because they were fleeing from the Americanos whom the Spaniards hate, they were willing to be led into that grim fortress of the white man.'

He made a little gesture.

'Perhaps it was as Forked Tongue promised. Perhaps we shall find they have been well-treated and fed, just as Forked Tongue said would be the case. And perhaps Forked Tongue's smooth, oily voice, has secured them sanctuary and benefits he spoke about!' Then Black Hawk paused before adding, sombrely, 'But it is in my heart to believe that Forked Tongue took them there with some idea of saving himself even at the cost of his own folks' lives.'

Black Hawk was shrewd. He had divined, in fact, the essence of Forked Tongue's strategy – Forked Tongue who could not bear to be a discredited man among his tribe, and who wanted only to get away from them and live in a place with wealth, where there was no danger and no more discomfort.

Forked Tongue was ever willing to betray his tribe if it would benefit himself . . . .

The Indians were on their feet when he had finished his story. They did not trust the Spaniard. They could understand the hunger which had gripped their womenfolk, and the ease with which they had been willing to believe Forked Tongue because of the crying of their children whose bellies were empty.

But now they wanted to go eastward along the plain to find their people, and if they could not rescue them from the hands of the ruthless, torturing Spaniard, they wanted to die with them.

But Black Hawk stayed them where they were. He told them of the man who had suddenly appeared from the bush.

'A Britisher,' he said, and he said it with something like confidence. Because it was well known that in Canada, where the British ruled, the red man was at peace and prospered alongside his white brother. There, there was justice for the red man, though in all this land of America outside Canada there was no justice at all for him.

When they heard that the Britisher had ridden eastwards to spy out the land and seek news of their people, they growled their pleasure. It was good to have an ally who was able to go into these places that weren't healthy for red men.

They lay down, after a while, to await the return of the white man. Not much later they began to hear sounds in the darkness, and that brought the redskins leaping to their feet.

They melted into the shadows of the bushes and listened, and then they realized that to the north of them men moved in stealthy fashion, and they were moving eastward. More, they seemed to be in force and once or twice in the distance they caught the glint of moonlight upon steel.

With bated breath these Indians remained where they were, until the men had passed. And then the Cherokees relaxed, and came gliding together and whispered.

Black Hawk was there to say at once, 'These are the American soldiers who fought against us. They have come through the swampland and now this can mean only one thing.'

They looked at him, for they knew that whatever it was this signified it would not be to the advantage of their people if they were within the fortress known to the Spaniards as Santa Maria.

Black Hawk said, 'This means that the Americans are going to attack the fortress.' He remembered those big guns on the horse-drawn limbers. 'They have mighty guns, powerful enough to blow holes through those thick walls. And if these Americans do take that fortress it means that, whatever the Spaniards' intentions, our people are doomed.'

They knew that Black Hawk was speaking the truth, and now they were silent and their faces were turned again towards the east.

There was the fortress and that way were their people. And silently stealing through the night towards them was this powerful body of American soldiery.

Again some wanted to move and go on after the soldiers and try to get to the fortress first and release their people, if it were at all possible.

But Black Hawk made them stay where they were. 'Soon we shall see that Britisher. He is our friend and he will advise us. He will come and tell us of the situation of our people, and he will advise us on our best course of action.'

Black Hawk suddenly had a great faith in that tall blue-eyed buck-skinned Britisher.

And then suddenly there was that Britisher before them. They heard the soft thud of hoofs upon hard-baked earth, and they crouched down because they were not to know the identity of the approaching horseman.

They saw him ride into the moonlit glade, and he was peering from under the broad brim of his hat, but his face was in the shadow.

So there was nothing else for it but to seize him quickly and quietly, in case he was not a friend. Running Elk came suddenly, swiftly leaping from out of the bushes and caught that gun hand before the rider, throwing himself from the saddle, could pull trigger.

And then Black Hawk was there to recognize his friend, and he was released, and they stood around him and everyone waited for the news that the white man would give them.

He drew in his breath and looked round at those silent, nearly naked, Indians in the darkness.

Then he said, 'O Redmen, I have found your people. They are prisoners in the fortress and there is a Cherokee who would sell them and other Indians into slavery.'

In the darkness there was a savage growl of hate and rage at the British hunter's words. They pressed round him, and their voices were quick to ask questions.

'A Cherokee?' It was Running Elk who asked that question, and for a man of good temper there was a lot of venom on his tongue. His big, ungainly form seemed to be towering into the night sky, as if he were about to burst with the rage that consumed him.

Jim Tyler shrugged. He said, 'He talked a lot. I think he was a warrior named Forked Tongue.'

Running Elk said, 'I think it could be no other Cherokee than that smooth-tongued serpent.'

Then Black Hawk said, 'We must save our people.'

Jim Tyler looked at the fine young warrior in that moonlight, and he thought of the Spanish garrison, now alerted by his visit.

They would be even more on their vigilance now that they had captured an American soldier, as was evidenced by that form that the Choctaw Indians had brought in.

He shook his head. 'You are few, Black Hawk. The Spaniards are many and they are behind a walled

fortress, and they have guns and many Indian merce-
naries to help them. I think you have no chance to
save your people.'

And then he told them something else.

'The American soldiers are creeping up on the
fortress.' He shrugged. 'True, they are as yet on
scouting expeditions, and might not attack the
fortress until daylight tomorrow. But it makes an
attempt to rescue your people even more hazardous.
You will not only have to fight the Spaniard and his
Indians, but that American army which has just
defeated the strength of your tribe.'

Those Indians grouped silently around him,
where he stood holding the head of his horse. And
then Running Elk, who had taken charge of the
warrior band because Chief Red Wolf had not
returned from the fighting, said tonelessly, 'They are
our people. While we have breath in our bodies we
must go to their aid. Even though it is death, we must
try to save them!'

At that there was a quick, savage murmur of
approval from that handful of braves. Jim Tyler
recognized the finality of the decision that was in
their mind, and he no longer tried to dissuade them.
Instead, he found admiration in his heart for these
people who could sacrifice themselves in a suicidal
attempt to help the weaker ones of their tribe.

He said softly, 'You are brave men. May the Great
Spirit go with you and be by your side when you
encounter your enemies.'

They parted soon after that. Tyler could not go with them, but he didn't say why he had to ride westwards. But he had to go because there was news that he was to telegraph out from some station in Laredo or Calveston. It was his duty to his government to let them know when situations such as this were developing on the American continent. For the British had a vital stake in the western hemisphere.

The Cherokees went eastward in single file, and they went like ghosts between those bushes, for if there were American scouts lying in them the Indians passed without being seen. They travelled at a pace which would have killed any ordinary man, but then they knew they were racing against time.

They were wise to the ways of the American troops, and they feared that at dawn those big guns would be ranged in position and hurling their cannon balls into the fortress. If they failed to rescue their people before the cordon of American troops closed in upon the fortress, and those whizzing red-hot balls crashed into the little town, then they knew they would never escape.

They had to rescue their people and get them away from the town under cover of darkness!

As they sped swiftly through the night, their eyes watched the eastern horizon. The stars told them that they still had two or three hours before daylight, but the way was long, and to their fanciful, fear-quickened imagination already they could see the eastern sky paling.

Lone Fern kept up with her menfolk. That was as they expected from an Indian maiden. If she felt weak and weary, she never showed it. When Black Hawk clumsily put out his hand to help her she shook it off for she knew that her warrior would have need of all his strength when they reached the town.

They must have passed right through any troops that were deployed towards the south of the town, and then all at once they were at the foot of the hill along whose ridge the massive fortress wall had been erected. They crouched in the bushes and looked at the serrated battlements outlined against an eastern sky which seemed lighter than it had been a few moments before.

There was a whispered colloquy, and then Black Hawk and two others went gliding like wraiths towards that wall on a scouting expedition. They had to find a way into the town.

They returned in a short while, though it seemed a desperately long time to the waiting Indians. They reported that the town was quiet again, as if the indolent Spaniards had been unable to resist the thought of sleep. But the sentries high up on the battlements were more alert than usual, and the Indians had heard them calling to each other, as if to keep themselves awake. Plainly the guards were nervous this night, as if not altogether dismissing the possibility of sudden attack.

The three Indian scouts said it would be possible for them to climb a part of the wall where a tree had fallen against it from some gale in time past. It was like a ladder to nimble-footed men, and only the soldiers of a decaying, crumbling empire would have tolerated its danger, leaning against the battlement wall.

One by one that tiny army of brave Indians ascended that sagging tree trunk and gained the high wall. Only Lone Fern remained behind. They dropped over into the shadow immediately beyond, and paused, crouching and watching on every side of them. They saw the silent ships, their tall masts reaching into that star-studded sky. They saw the moon reflecting upon waters which looked oily and vaguely treacherous to these Indians from the great plains of America.

And they looked upon the reed huts and the crude timber-and-'dobe dwellings of the poor people, who lived within the battlement walls for safety – and found little in the mercy of their Spanish masters.

But the Indians were more interested in that tall, sombre blockhouse that was the main fort, and in these battlemented walls along which dark shadows of Spanish sentries patrolled.

Here was the menace. These wakeful eyes might see them, and might raise the alarm and bring about their downfall before they had a chance to liberate their people.

Black Hawk glided away and none followed, for they knew what the tall warrior was intent on doing.

He moved from shadow to shadow, like a shadow himself, until he was within a yard of a sentry who peered fearfully into the night, and never thought that danger might leap up behind.

Black Hawk reached out and his hand gripped and the man stiffened and struggled, but when his rifle fell Black Hawk's bare leg kicked out and neatly caught it in the crook of his foot, and it made no sound.

And that sentry made no sound, either.

Black Hawk gave the chirrup of a tree cricket, and yet with all those real tree crickets chirruping, the ears of his friends heard it and understood and they stole silently along the wall after him. When they reached that stricken sentry, they found Black Hawk had gone, and with him was the rifle and ammunition of the fallen man.

There were three more sentries along that wall until they reached the ladder that went down by the gate. Three sentries – and all looked out over the plain where it was reported American soldiers were gathering. And none of them saw Black Hawk, and all fell to him without a sound.

Then those lithe Indians swarmed down the ladder and softly crept up to the one building in the courtyard which was bathed in lamplight. They peered inside. The rest of the guards were sleeping, all except a guard commander, who had been lashed for letting a prisoner escape.

He was writhing as he tried to find comfort in lying

on the bed that was always allotted to a prisoner; for his indolence had made him a prisoner this night, too.

He saw ghosts rise out of the moonlit plaza, and then his eyes widened with terror for those ghosts, like great timber wolves, were within that guard-room and they went each to a man . . . and no man moved thereafter.

That guard commander failed to move again, too.

Now those Cherokees had no more fatigue and weariness in their bones. Success was as heady as wine to them, and they lusted to be within that block-house, where they thought they would find their people. They looked at the sky and to themselves swore that dawn was at hand, and yet even if it was they could not turn back now without going through with their mission.

They went towards a door which would have been kept locked and bolted and barred at nights by a man worthy of the name of fort commandant. But still it was open because the fort commandant liked a breeze circulating in the upper region, where he slept in a bed of fine linen that had been made by Indian squaw women who were his slaves.

Those dozen Indians went within. Two melted into the darkness on either side of the door and remained there to guard the retreat of their fellows. The others flitted from one rounded archway to another, gently trying door handles, and finally finding that all were locked.

They silently ascended the winding stone stairway down which Jim Tyler had so recently leapt to freedom. And when they were out on that moonlit passage, they went from door to door and tried them, and where the doors were unlocked they went inside and . . . and anyone they found a-bed died where they lay.

Black Hawk went to the biggest door. It was unlocked, and even slightly ajar, to permit of that circulating breeze. Black Hawk silently went within.

He found himself in a majestic room which was open to the night air where wide windows gave out on to a balcony. There was a sleeper in a bed in a shadowy corner, but he didn't see it and he failed to detect the sounds of heavy breathing, and went over to that balcony, his quick eyes darting from shadow to shadow, so as to detect any possible lurking enemies.

He looked out over the night scene in the tiny harbour, and he was turning, when suddenly he realized where his people were being kept prisoner.

The thin wailing cry of a child, disturbed in its sleep, rose to his ears. At once he went forward, his hands resting on the top of the balcony balustrade. He looked down, and his keen eyes saw all that he needed to see in that vivid moonlight.

He looked down the face of a precipice that was broken by a wide shelf about forty yards below him on his right. On this shelf he saw huddled figures in sleep, all except for one – a woman – who was sitting upright and rocking and speaking softly to hush her child, clasped in her arms. And Black Hawk detected immediately that that voice was speaking in Cherokee – more, he even thought that he knew the woman.

Exulting, he turned to go out into the passage and tell his comrades what he had seen. Then he saw a movement.

Someone had been wakened by that child's cry, and had turned and seen the menacing silhouette of that mighty Indian warrior standing on the moonlit balcony.

The Spanish commandant was out of his bed and into the middle of the room in an instant, clad in his nightshirt. He looked a ridiculous figure, but Black Hawk had no thought of ridicule; for he saw in this long-faced, pointed-bearded white man a threat to their entire expedition just at a time when it seemed they might have success.

The moonlight fell full upon that sharp-featured face, and Black Hawk saw the widening brown eyes, and the little cavern of a mouth begin to open blackly in that Spaniard's face, preparatory to giving a warning cry.

Black Hawk rushed across the room in one tremendous leap. He made a noise, but not too much noise, and in any event Black Hawk had no alternative.

That opening mouth had to be silenced before a cry could be uttered!

105

Those strong, sinewy hands fell upon the throat of the Spaniard, and then the crushing weight of the Indian's body felled the commandant. For a few seconds there was a frantic struggle for life on the floor against the big carved wooden bed.

And then the fort commandant was still and the danger was over . . . .

Black Hawk rose and went out into the passage, and at once his brothers came gliding up to meet him. He whispered that he had found his people but he did not know how to get to them.

His sharp mind guessed that a tunnel or passageway must lead from the fortress, built upon this rocky cliff; down to that ledge so convenient for keeping prisoners. But they had no time to look for it. To their anxious minds dawn seemed imminent any moment now.

Black Hawk wheeled and went back into the commandant's quarters. He tore the clothes off the bed and ripped them down the middle and began to knot them together. His companions saw the plan in his mind, and with feverish intensity assisted him in his work.

They tied one end of the improvised rope to the balcony stonework. And then the fluttering white rope was dropped, and Black Hawk immediately went over the balcony and, in the full light of that betraying moon, began to swarm down to the end of the rope.

When he reached it he found he was ten yards

from the end of the tapering ledge.

He twisted, hanging on to that rope, and looking down into the void below where certain death awaited him if he made any incautious movement.

And then he started to walk with his feet along the wall in an effort to get himself swinging like a pendulum. He heard the bed-clothes creak as they tightened and lengthened, and once there was a little movement and he dropped a few inches as if a knot had slipped.

But he kept on swinging. The lives of his people depended on his and his comrades' actions now. When he was swinging in a wide arc, pendulum fashion, he waited for the downward rush to end and then he let go of the rope. For one instant he was flying through mid-air, and then his feet stubbed on to that narrow ledge, and he was staggering to try to recover his balance.

His foot slipped off the edge, and he found himself falling. Desperately he flung out his hands, and they grasped the crumbling stone edge of that long broadening edge. He paused for a second to regain his breath, and then with a mighty heave of shoulders strengthened by combat and hazardous hunting expeditions, he dragged himself on to that shelf.

When he looked, he saw that a companion had already descended and was at the end of the rope.

But it was easier for his brothers. He was there to catch the second man as he flew across the gap, and

107

that second man was able to help the third man, and so on.

But Black Hawk didn't wait for his comrades to follow him. He glided along that ledge, towards where the prisoners lay back against the cliff wall. He saw a light, suddenly, as he rounded a protruberance on the cliff face. There was a place here hacked squarely out of the rock, and it seemed to be a gaol-house, for there was an oil lamp on a table, and two or three men sat around it. And behind them was a barred door that looked like a cell in which very dangerous prisoners might be kept.

But Black Hawk wasn't looking at the cell. He was looking at the enemy – those jailers. There could be no release of his people until they were silenced.

His eyes for a moment flickered away from them, and he saw that a shaft led from this gaolhouse, and he guessed that it gave access to within the fort.

He waited now until three other comrades joined him. They whispered that the rest had stayed above to guard their retreat. But Black Hawk thought there could be no retreat. Because it did not seem possible for them to return the way they had come.

Death was their lot for certain if their plans miscar-ried now!

The four Indians moved across to those dozing men at the table. And then Black Hawk's leg brushed against something that was like a thread, stretched across the lamplit gaolhouse. At once a metal pan, or something of that nature, clattered off a low shelf.

The guards were alerted immediately.

Their warning device had served them well, and now they were lurching to their feet, their startled eyes upon that quartet of crouching Indians, their hands diving for the guns they carried in their belts.

Four lithe warriors spurned dust with their moccasined feet as they leapt in desperate endeavour to silence these guards. They moved so fast, the guards were caught before they could utter a sound.

Black Hawk was upon the biggest of the trio, and his hand grasped across a face that was stiff with beard. Then the man, big though he was, was raised off his feet, and then lowered to the ground, and Black Hawk was kneeling upon him . . . .

When he rose his comrades were rising from their opponents, too.

They went to where their people were. It was a moment of joy such as they had never expected to know.

Those prisoners woke and their astonished eyes fell upon faces they had never expected to see again. They were on their feet in a moment, and some of the women were weeping, and they were touching the warriors and stroking them, in their excess of emotion at the meeting.

Black Hawk got them together, and there were a full eighty of them. He heard babies begin to cry, and his heart seemed to stop at the sound, but there was nothing he could do about it.

The warriors looked among their people for a

sight of Forked Tongue, but he was not there.

Brown Otter, a comrade of Black Hawk who had been with the women and old men because his shoulder was shattered by a bullet during the earlier fighting, explained, 'He was taken away by the guards during the night. He did not return.'

Black Hawk's eyes were molten with anger as he said, 'He went to make trade with the white man. He would have you sold into slavery, and sell Creeks and Seminoles, too.'

But there was no time for talk about their traitor. Black Hawk turned and leapt into the gaolhouse again. He found keys on the body of the biggest of the guards, and with them in his hand he ran back up the sloping passageway until he found himself at the foot of a long flight of steps. It took him but a few moments to climb them, and then he was faced by a massive iron-studded door. The bolts were off, however, and there was only the lock to open.

He inserted the key, and gently turned it, so as to make as little noise as possible. And then he pulled on the big iron ring that was set in the door for a handle.

And the door remained closed against him. It had been bolted from the outside.

9

THE WAY IS BARRED!

Black Hawk turned and raced back on to the ledge again. He saw the faces of his people and they were desperate with anxiety now. But he could give them no reassurance. He crossed to the edge of that wide shelf, and as he ran his eyes were on the east and he knew now that this was no imagination, but there was a growing light distantly.

Now they had minutes only before dawn came and that little town, still nestling in sleep, stirred and began to go about its daily activities. When that happened they were doomed. That large party of women and children and aged and disabled could never flee fast enough to save themselves from the vengeful Spaniard and his allies.

Desperately Black Hawk turned to look at the cliff

111

face around them. But it was unscalable. There was
no way off this ledge, apparently, and in fact they had
just obligingly added themselves to the Spaniards'
prisoners.

For one second a wave of despair swept over the
warrior. Was this to be the end of that mission which
had gone so well until now? Were they to be defeated
in the end because one door stood between them
and a chance of a break for freedom?

A mighty rage seemed to consume the warrior at
that. He looked at those pleading faces of those
women and their children. And he thought, 'By the
Great Spirit I will yet find a way out of this trap!'

He ran back to the end of that narrow ledge and
he looked across and saw the rope of bedclothes
swinging in the gentle night breeze. He looked at the
distance between himself and the end of it, and his
heart almost stopped.

It was an impossible jump. No man could leap that
far and still live . . . .

His eyes suddenly hardened. And then he began
to calculate. For he realized that occasionally the
wind blew stronger and at such times that long rope
swung perhaps as much as three feet nearer to the
ledge than when it was stationary. Then it was just
possible that a mighty leaper could jump across that
yawning gulf and grasp the rope before he fell to his
death.

Black Hawk went back twenty yards along the
ledge, and the eyes of his people were upon him, for

they knew now what was in his mind, and they feared it was a feat beyond any man.

Black Hawk hesitated, and in his mind was the thought, 'If I do leap that gulf will the rope stand my sudden weight upon it?'

At that moment he became conscious of the brightening light. Very soon now the first rays of Florida sunshine would be warming the chill morning air and bringing the people uncomfortably from their blankets.

That was enough for Black Hawk. He began to race forward. He put everything he had into that mighty run-up, and then into the tremendous leap off the crumbling edge of that narrow shelf. He had estimated well. He leapt on to that rope just at the moment when it was at the maximum of its swing.

His fingers grasped – slipped – and grasped again. He heard the rope creak, and he swung wildly into space, but then his heart beat gladly, for he realized it would hold.

He heard the gasp from his people back on the ledge, and then, as he swung and started to climb hand over hand up towards that balcony, he heard the thrilled murmur as their hopes began to rise again.

Black Hawk went up that rope like lightning. Now it was a frantic race against sunshine, and they had too little time.

His comrades helped him over the balcony, but he

did not stay but plunged across towards the passage way, whispering quickly an explanation.

'A door bars our way to freedom. We must find that door!'

He had a good idea where he would find the door, and they went down the curving stone stairway towards the hall.

It was still dim within this hall, because the only light came in from the open doorway. The Indians looked into one arched doorway after another. Several were locked. They were approaching one, when it opened in their faces.

Petrified they halted where they were. A Spanish servant came through the door. He was carrying a hot drink – probably coffee – for his master. It was on a tray and there were lots of silverware and pieces of china.

He stepped into the hall and saw himself faced by nearly a dozen warriors, and the tray dropped from his hands immediately.

One of the Indians made a frantic effort to catch it before it clattered to the stone-flagged hallway. The rest of his brothers swarmed on to that hapless Spaniard.

But the tray slipped through those eager, grasping fingers, and fell with a shattering sound on to the floor.

The Indians looked at each other, horrified for one second. Then Black Hawk whispered, 'There is nothing we can do about it, brothers. Keep watch, and let us try and find that door.'

The Indians leapt to positions alongside every doorway inside that big hall, and two went running back up the stairs and hid at the top in case people from above became alarmed.

And then they found the door. There was one which was barred on the outside. Black Hawk leapt across and dragged back the bolts and flung open the door and looked down upon a familiar staircase.

He left his comrades to keep watch while he raced down those steps and along the passageway into the jailhouse.

As he came out on to the shelf again, his eyes were on the eastern horizon and he saw yellow rays beginning to climb over the curving blue skyline. Dawn was breaking!

He led those people up the long passageway, and up those tedious steps. His ears were straining for sounds from the hallway which would say that they had been discovered and the door was being slammed and locked in their faces. That would have been unendurable.

But no one had been disturbed by that shattering crockery and that clanging metal tray.

Black Hawk came leaping up the stairs and saw his comrades there, and they were plain to be seen now because the morning sun was dissipating the shadows within those Moorish archways. They stood aside and watched the frantic women hurrying in with their children clasped to them. He saw the old men being helped by warriors lame and hurt themselves, but still capable of giving aid to the aged.

The warriors drew together as the people came silently up that stairway. Black Hawk said, 'We have no time for anything but bold action.'

They did not understand what he meant, but their trust was in this warrior who had been so brave and resourceful and had saved his people.

He went to the big door and looked out. The sunshine was warm and yellow now upon the mighty fortress gates, where sentries no longer stood on watch.

Down below from the little township, came the thin call of a child, up early and out to play. The world was waking. They hadn't a minute to spare.

Black Hawk turned and said to his people, 'We will be bold. Let us go across this open yard before us and risk being seen by anyone who is out of bed. Let us open the main gate and run out into the freedom beyond.'

There was a murmur of approval. Their situation was desperate and they seemed to have no alternative.

Black Hawk and his warriors sped across the warming, sunlit plaza, and passed the silent guardroon and came to the unguarded main gate. The Indians looked at the fastenings of the gate, and then saw there was a small wicket door set into the main gates. There were massive iron bars holding it fast, and it was the work of seconds only for the Indians to lift the bars and begin to drag open that little, creaking door.

Down below in the town, a woman's scolding voice became added to that of the playing child. Within seconds now, perhaps, someone would be coming up to the gateway on his way out to the world beyond.

The frightened Indian children and their mothers came flooding across to where that wicket gate was opening. Black Hawk heard the sharp intake of breaths behind him, and knew the fear that consumed them.

He dragged open the gate . . . .

And then gently he closed it again. He looked round upon his people and his eyes were agonized. There was no escape that way!

For, trained upon the fortress gate, was a line of American artillery. And ranged behind the big guns and on either side of them were the blue-coated United States cavalry and infantry.

10

FORKED TONGUE!

He didn't make any explanation. But they knew by his expression that their way of escape was barred. What they didn't know was that a peril had been added to all others. Now it was not just a race against time and against detection, but against being caught in the full blast of another enemy's fire – an enemy more formidable than any they had had to face this night.

But Black Hawk was determined to escape. He had not come so far and suffered so much only to see the cup of success dashed from his lips right at the last moment.

He looked at the ladder which led up to the ramparts, and he thought of that tree which was like a ladder a quarter of a mile to the south of them. That tree was right over the wall at a point where the town lay. If they were to use it as a way of escape, they would have to walk in full view of the stirring town,

high up on the battlements, approaching the buildings all the while.

But there was no other way of escape for them that
Black Hawk could see. He ran across to that broad,
primitive ladder which was a thing of struts, and
sinews to hold them together. He went first, because
there might be danger ahead. And then the womenfolk followed their children, and behind them their
aged and wounded. The other warriors remained to
the last, to fight if enemies stirred.

It took a long while for them to climb that
awkward ladder, and they were so many, and most
were weak and needed support or assistance.

But there came a time when all of them were up
on the ramparts, and streaming in a quick little
procession behind that hurrying figure of the mighty
Black Hawk.

He wanted to run, the urgency of the moment
gripping him, but he knew his people could not keep
up with him. But he kept hurrying ahead, and then
gesturing to encourage them to follow, waiting until
they caught up with him and then going ahead
again.

He was gripping that rifle he had taken from the
first sentry, and his fingers were on the lock, while his
eyes looked down into that town. They were coming
nearer, descending that wall which ran down the hillside, until they were walking right above the reed
roofs and shingles of the poor habitations.

And people were walking about now. Not many,

but women were going out to fetch water. Children were playing. And bare-legged fishermen were going down to where their boats were drawn up on the golden sands. More and more people were stirring and could be heard talking sleepily and even quarrelling within those houses.

High above the wakening town, clearly seen on those cat-walks along the ramparts of the great fortress wall, moved that silent, terrified procession of Indians. And yet no man's eyes were turned to look up to them. No one saw them.

His heart in his mouth, Black Hawk watched, his eyes like an eagle's darting from one unsuspecting Spaniard to another. His gun was ready to fire, but seconds passed, and they came nearer to where the leafy top of the tree stood above the parapet, and there was no need for gunplay.

And then when the leading women were no more than fifty yards from that ladder to safety, a child began to wail in terror.

It made a great noise, and to their frantic ears, it seemed a tremendous disturbance. And yet there is no way of keeping a child quiet and they knew it, and they had to hurry on while that noise rang disturbingly around them.

Black Hawk stood under the tree and watched in agony, and he saw that his people were stretched for a good hundred and fifty yards back along the wall, and it would take minutes for them all to get down to that tree.

His braves were racing towards him now, because they would have to go and position themselves along that tree trunk and help down the weaker of their tribe.

The first of them went over. To Black Hawk's eager ears he heard a glad cry. Lone Fern was still waiting for them at the foot of the tree.

Black Hawk took the first child and handed it to a warrior who was on the wall. He handed that child on to a man lower down in the tree and that warrior passed it on until it was carried to the bottom. Lone Fern took the child and began to hurry away with it.

The nimbler of the young women went down the tree without difficulty, and their children were passed after them, especially that crying, terrified child.

Black Hawk looked over the town and still no one looked up at them and they were safe. And then he risked a glance westwards, across the prairie where the American armies were ranged.

His heart sank because he saw that though they could escape from this fortress, they would only run into the lines of American soldiers who seemed to stretch right down to the seashore.

But those blue uniforms were a good mile or more distant, and there might be gaps in the line, and they might escape through with their lives.

The first thing was for them to escape from this dangerous position, and then to worry about the danger beyond!

The sun was hot above the horizon now, and the whole world was light and warm. The Spanish flag fluttered on the mast on the tower of the fortress.

They were winning, Black Hawk thought. They would get out of this prison fortress with their lives after all, he was thinking. It began to seem as though those heedless people, concerned about their early morning activities in the town below, would never think to look in their direction, and they would escape with ease.

He even found time to talk to Brown Otter, who stood aside as a warrior should to let the weaker ones go ahead of him. Though Brown Otter was weak because of loss of blood following that smashed shoulder.

And Brown Otter was saying that Black Hawk was a man among men. That night his bravery would live for ever in the annals of the Cherokee nation. He did not add 'what is left of them'.

He seemed not at all surprised when Black Hawk told him that the American enemy was outside and about to open fire upon the fortress.

He seemed to know that they were there, and that was a surprise to Black Hawk. And then Brown Otter, watching their people still streaming up to clamber over the wall and down towards at least a temporary safety, said, 'They brought in an American soldier last night. Some hunting Choctaws ran across him and they brought him back to their Spanish masters.'

There was contempt in his voice as he finished his

sentence, as if he thought nothing of Indians who
served a white tyrant.

They stood and gave help where they could, and
they fretted because those old people seemed so slow
in going down that ladder to freedom. There were
still fifty at least of their people to descend, and it was
taking far longer than Black Hawk had thought.

The sun was hot upon them now. And then they
heard men shouting and the voices came from up at
the fortress.

Their eyes flickered uneasily down into the town,
and they marvelled because even now no one
seemed to look their way.

But it was evident that it wouldn't be long before
those people who had stumbled upon the tragedy of
the fortress, came running down into the town to
give the alarm.

Desperately they hauled people on to the wall and
got them moving down to safety. And yet there were
still forty to go.

Brown Otter was talking now as if to try to keep
from his thoughts the possibility of imminent detection. For they were easy targets, high up on that wall,
to people with guns and even bows and arrows below.

He was saying. 'He was an infantryman. A man
who fought upon his feet and not his horse.' He
made a careful explanation of the distinction. 'His
hair was red and his face was red, and he had big
hands, and he was as strong as any man I have seen.
For when they tried to put him in that cell he broke

his bonds and lashed out and made unconscious several of his enemies. He was shouting that he was not a real soldier, but was on his way to send a report through to a newspaper.'

Brown Otter knew what a newspaper was. He was an intelligent man and had lived with white people in the towns of Georgia, and had thought himself their friend until this final act of treachery when they had been driven from the lands they occupied.

He was talking on, but he hadn't seen the expression in his companion's face. For a picture had leapt into Black Hawk's mind as Brown Otter's voice nade his explanation. He was seeing that infantryman in that description, the man who had saved his life at the risk of his own.

Brown Otter heard him say: 'This red-haired man, where did they put him?'

Brown Otter said: 'He was inside that cell with the door with the bars of iron.'

Black Hawk thought, 'I was near to that man who befriended me, and yet I did not know it, and I left him to his fate!'

Because the Spaniards were known to kill all their prisoners if there was a chance that they might be rescued by an enemy.

But there was nothing he could do about it for the moment. There were his people still to get down that ladder. Below, they were being led away into the shelter of bushes, though how long there would be protection for them when the American soldiers advanced they did not know. But it was sufficient for the moment.

There were twenty people only on that wall when suddenly it seemed that the skies were rent asunder. There was a mighty crashing sound as a battery of guns fired a salvo, and their whizzing cannon balls pounded holes into the 'dobe walls of that fortress.

Dust flew everywhere, and there were screams and shouts from the startled people below. And then their eyes came naturally round to look at that wall beyond which the cannon roar had come. They saw the fleeing Indians outlined against the ramparts in the brilliant morning sunshine.

Black Hawk urged them over the wall now in a frantic endeavour to get them out of sight of the guns of those people down below. His own gun was lifted to his shoulder, and when he saw a man run into the open carrying a gun he fired and sent him sprawling on his face.

Black Hawk quickly reloaded. His other braves began to fire now as more people ran out with weapons. Some were Indians, and just as much to be feared with their bows and arrows as the Spaniards with their clumsy, muzzle-loading guns.

They knelt on the ramparts, and kept the startled citizens of Santa Maria in hiding, and with every second that passed, more of their people clambered over the wall into safety.

And there came a time when the last wounded warrior was being helped down, and then Black

Hawk's braves began to descend that tree like lithe pumas.

The cannons crashed another mighty salvo into the fortress walls. Spanish soldiers were coming out from their barrack rooms, and scaling the ladder and getting into position along the ramparts. Black Hawk saw a group racing towards him along the cat-walk, their guns pointing and their voices shouting in anger at him.

He saw the last of his comrades go over.

On the outside of the fortress wall his braves gathered at the foot of the tree and waited for him to come over. He did not come in sight. They looked at each other then, and said: 'He must have been shot. In his hour of victory, Black Hawk, mightiest of our warriors, must have died!'

It put an end to that wild exultation they had been feeling, and they turned and loped into the bushes in silence after their people. They found them strung out in a long line, being led ever into the thickest parts of this scrub-covered plain.

Lone Fern was hanging back now, wanting to see Black Hawk again and be assured of his safety. When she saw the warriors racing up to join their people, and Black Hawk was not with them, her face became rigid with fear. And then she turned without a word, and went to help a woman who was overburdened with children. It was not in the code of an Indian to betray sorrow even though it was there . . . .

Black Hawk deliberately leapt from the wall and

126

sought the cover of those crowding reed huts below. There were many who saw him and began to run to find him and slay him out of hand.

But Black Hawk was bold and resourceful, and he leapt into the nearest hut and dashed through it before anyone had time to come round behind them. He ran out on to an ascending pathway, and at once found himself among other Indians, though these were Choctaws who had given their freedom for the protection of the Spanish conqueror.

There was such confusion, and so many Indians racing out of huts and running up towards the fortress, that no one noticed Black Hawk, though those Choctaws should have detected one who was not of their tribe.

So it was that Black Hawk ran, right amidst his enemies, while an astonished search party beat around the huts where they had last seen him, and failed to find him.

Black Hawk's grim eyes watched that fortress as the party ran up. There was confusion such as he had never seen before, and this would be because the Spaniards had lost their commandant, and so far there was no one solely in charge.

The Spaniards, some wearing the old-fashioned metal breast-plates of the Conquistadores, were shouting and pointing to the ramparts. They were urging the Indians to go up, to be in position to make a defence when the American infantry came in after the bombardment. Every minute or so those mighty guns would boom out, there on the plain, and then balls of red-hot iron would whistle over the wall and crash into a 'dobe fortress which was already crumbling.

It had not been designed to stand an assault on this scale, and it was apparent to the defenders of Fortress Santa Maria that the blockhouse would not stand up to such treatment for long. It turned out to be in Black Hawk's favour.

For the building had been evacuated, no one daring to stay within the target of that battery of guns, expertly handled by the American artillery-men.

Black Hawk ran through the dust which billowed out as part of the 'dobe wall collapsed beneath the bombardment. No one saw him enter by those familiar wide-open doors – if they did, no one thought any more about it.

Inside the large hall, he found the place in a shambles. Parts of the ceiling had collapsed, and a wall hung drunkenly in a position which threatened a fall at the next salvo. Black Hawk climbed over the debris, searching for that door which led down to the jailhouse and praying that it would not be locked and the keys be missing.

He tried the door when he came up to it, and to his delight it swung open. At that moment a mighty roar told of a further hit by those canon balls. Great chunks of 'dobe crashed down around him, and dust rose so that for a few seconds he could not see more than a yard or so. He reeled as the earth shook and the whole building seemed to tremor on its foundations. Then he slammed back the door and raced down the staircase and then down a sloping passageway to where the prisoners had been kept.

Now the place seemed deserted. Deserted, that is, save for three sprawling figures who had once been jailers.

Black Hawk ran across towards that massive door set into the rock face of this jailhouse. He saw movement in the dark interior as he came up, and he realized that a prisoner was gripping those bars and staring out at him.

He ran up, and then he saw that the prisoner was indeed the American who had saved his life.

The red-haired American recognized him, and must have realized instinctively that Black Hawk had come back in a desperate effort to save him. He shouted, 'Good for you, brother! Maybe you can settle scores a bit now!'

Black Hawk tried the door, but it was locked, and there was no key in it, and there was no key anywhere to be seen, in fact. He searched the bodies of those jailers, and then he ran back up to the door that led out to that main hall, but someone had taken the keys out of the lock. He went back then to the prisoner, and told him that he couldn't find the keys that would release him.

Another crashing salvo brought dust swirling down the passageway as more of the fortress collapsed. It was only a question of time now before the building came down completely. If that happened, and the passageway to freedom was blocked, they would be in a bad position. It might be, in fact, that they would be trapped and left to die before anyone could get to their assistance.

That red-haired American in the blue uniform pressing against his cell door, must have realized this, for he changed his tune now, shouting, 'You look after yourself. You can't help me, so get away as fast as your legs will take you. Get out of here before the whole darn place comes toppling in on us!'

But that was a thought far from Black Hawk's mind. He owed a debt to this American, and he intended to repay it. He would not leave this place while there was a possibility of saving his benefactor's life. He picked up a gun that had been the jailer's, and he smashed the heavy butt against the door . . . and the gun butt splintered and broke in two. It would take a lot to batter that door down.

So again Black Hawk went up those stairs, but there was no thought in his mind of saving his own skin. Somewhere someone had the keys to this cell, and he intended to find them.

A man leapt on to him as he came up the sloping passageway towards the foot of the stairs.

Black Hawk was taken completely by surprise, and he went rolling backwards, the rough stone tearing at his naked shoulders as he fell.

He found himself lying, his arms gripped, and he

saw a knife lifted to plunge into his heart.

And he saw the face behind that knife, and it was Forked Tongue's.

11

THE DANGER.

Black Hawk rolled, and in the same instant he exerted all his strength and tore his arms free, and in the same movement crashed his fist out and knocked away the descending knife arm.

In a savage fury he rolled again and fought to free himself. His fist crashed into the naked ribs of this man who thought more of himself than the weak ones of his tribe. Time and again Black Hawk crashed home his fist, and all the time he struggled madly to get from under the treacherous brave and free himself.

They rolled together, fighting like mountain cats, until they came out on to that broad shelf right under the gaze of the helpless American prisoner.

Then Black Hawk hit his opponent on the side of his head and knocked him over. By the time Forked Tongue had recovered his spinning senses, Black

Hawk had thrown him away, and was on his feet, swaying and panting, his eyes glittering murderously at this man he hated.

Forked Tongue had lost his knife during the tumble down the sloping passageway, but he seized it again and with the same movement came with a mighty bound at Black Hawk. The warrior saw that fiendishly hateful face of the renegade Cherokee, and before he could get his own knife he realized that Forked Tongue would stab the heart out of him.

So Black Hawk crashed forward like a mighty buffalo, and his body went under the knife blow, and smashed into Forked Tongue's exposed chest.

Forked Tongue fell backwards, hitting the floor so hard that for seconds he was dazed and could hardly move.

And in that time Black Hawk was able to see that the Cherokee was carrying a ring of keys from a cord around his waist. For some reason Forked Tongue had secured possession of those keys and had been on his way perhaps to release the American prisoner in order to get into favour with these attacking Americanos.

That was the kind of man Forked Tongue was. He liked to think ahead, and to take such actions as were designed to protect his own worthless life.

Black Hawk went streaking across to grasp those keys. Forked Tongue saw him coming and suddenly kicked out. Black Hawk felt the pain as that foot crashed into his face. He reeled and went over sideways. While he was trying to stagger up from the ground, Forked Tongue was on to him again, snarling and trying to put a rope round Black Hawk's neck and strangle him.

Black Hawk turned, just in time, and flung out his hand and stopped Forked Tongue's headlong, reckless flight in a painful way. Now it was Forked Tongue's turn to feel pain in his face and to fall back dizzily.

Then the two leapt together again, and they fought, and now each was fighting to get his hands upon the other's throat and choke the life out of him. For this could only be a fight to the death.

Dimly Black Hawk realized that the firing was continuing, that cannon balls were rocking this fortress to the foundation, and any moment the whole building might collapse in on top of them.

He also realized that above the roar of those cannons firing, and the crashing sounds as more and more wall toppled in, the American prisoner was shouting at him.

He didn't know what the American was saying. But it seemed to him to be frantic – to be trying to tell him something.

All at once he realized what the American was trying to warn him against.

Suddenly his legs swung into space. He released his hold on Forked Tongue, and grasped frantically at the edge of this shelf. Without realizing it they rolled almost into space over the end of this prison ledge.

Forked Tongue exulted, seeing a momentary advantage. His fist pounded savagely at Black Hawk's extended, clawing fingers, trying to make him release his hold. He tried to kick Black Hawk in the chest and send him hurtling down into those tremendous depths below.

But Black Hawk suddenly shifted his grip and grabbed that extended leg, and now if Forked Tongue sent Black Hawk to his death, Black Hawk was going to take his enemy with him.

With a convulsive heave Black Hawk somehow got his leg on to the ledge again, and carried himself a couple of yards into safety. Forked Tongue came staggering to his feet. Black Hawk fell rather than leapt forward, and his falling fists fell full upon that savage face, and Forked Tongue went reeling backwards.

Forked Tongue desperately swung on his toes to minimise the crushing effect of that mighty blow. His foot seemed to slip, as if he went off his balance with the suddenness of the movement.

And then Black Hawk, falling on to his knees with the impetus of his movement, saw his enemy topple over the edge of the cliff. Forked Tongue hadn't realized that he was so near to danger himself, and Black Hawk had an impression of his enemy's face filling with surprise that he had miscalculated so. That expression gave way to panic and the most awful of terrors. Forked Tongue went spinning down into the depths, and his scream rose to Black Hawk's ears as he went over.

FORTRESS SANTA MARIA

There was no escape for Forked Tongue from that fall. Below – too far below for a man to fall and survive – was the hard, cobbled paving of an alleyway that led around the rear of the town. Forked Tongue crashed on to it and was still for ever more.

Black Hawk reared to his feet, his mighty lungs seeking the air they needed after that frantic struggle for life. And his eyes sought the American's helplessly. They said, 'I tried to help, but I failed.'

For Forked Tongue had had those keys to the prison attached round his waist, and now his broken body was lying at the foot of the precipice.

There was a feeling as of an earthquake, as another salvo brought a floor down, and great boulders of 'dobe walling came toppling on to the ledge, to smash into fragments and fill the space where the prisoner had been with a choking dust-cloud. The tremoring continued, as if the whole building was now shifting and steadily collapsing.

The rattle of the musket fire along the outer wall seemed to fade away at that, as if sight of the blockhouse disintegrating knocked the thought of further resistance out of the defenders' minds. Then as the dust began to clear a little, Black Hawk realized that the American was shaking furiously at the bar of his door, and was shouting to him.

Black Hawk went over to him, his shoulders drooping because it seemed there was no chance for this helpless American. But then that red-haired, grey-eyed American was shouting, 'There they are!

136

There!' And his finger was stabbing through the bars and pointing. Black Hawk swung round in the direction of that pointing finger. He saw something glistening bright among the debris, and he picked it up and it was a ring with keys on it.

Then he saw a rope – the rope that Forked Tongue had tried to use as a garrotte with which to strangle him. Forked Tongue must have whipped off the rope from around his waist for that purpose, and in so doing he had dropped the keys from it.

Black Hawk raced to the cell and tried the keys and at last found one that fitted, and he heard the crude iron latch jump back. The door swung open. The man in the blue uniform of an American soldier came striding out. He said nothing in the way of thanks, but he clasped his hands around Black Hawk's mighty bare shoulders, and seemed to hug him for a brief second.

Then Black Hawk turned, and began to race up the passageway. He heard the pounding boots of the American behind him, and then they came to the stairs – and stopped.

The way was blocked. That last salvo had brought debris crashing through the doorway and filling the upper part of the staircase.

Black Hawk hesitated for only a second, and then he went clambering forward, climbing over that debris. When he was over the top of the door, crouched frog-like because the roof was low, he began to tear at the boulders that stood between them and freedom. Behind him worked the American, panting as he strove to throw still farther back the debris that this mighty Indian tossed about as if they were child's things.

Again they heard the roar of cannons and felt the impact as the balls smote into the reeling fortress. There was a further outbreak of thundering roaring, as another part of the blockhouse collapsed. And then they heard men shouting frantically, and it seemed to them that these voices were calling upon other defenders to yield to this all-powerful enemy who was at their gates.

The sound made Black Hawk redouble his effort. If he were found in the act of leaving this blockhouse by American soldiers just pouring into the fortress, there was little doubt that he would be shot on sight.

As he threw back a boulder he grunted to the American, 'The general will kill you if he sees you?'

The American shoved back more debris and nodded. But he seemed quite cool about it. He said, 'Maybe he will. General Jackson's a pretty direct man. Though he's got no authority to hang me, because I am a civilian.'

They slung back more debris. Now Black Hawk could see the doorway. In a few minutes, unless there was a further fall of walling, they would be able to crawl out.

The Indian heard his American friend say: 'That's true, Black Hawk. I am a civilian, I carried a rifle for self-protection, but I never once used it against your people. This expedition of General Jackson's been wrong right from its start. I want to get word through to my editor about these goings on. General Jackson's taken the law into his own hands.'

Black Hawk didn't understand. All he knew was that ever since he'd been a child, the Americans had been taking the law into their own hands.

He put his mighty shoulders to the task of heaving on a slab of 'dobe. It broke in half, and went clattering down into the hallway, and now there was enough room for them both to crawl through.

Panting, Black Hawk got down on to his stomach and dragged himself through, pulling his rifle with him as he did so. The American came out hard on his heels.

When they were in the shattered hallway, a final salvo seemed to send the whole of the structure tottering backwards towards the precipice on whose edge it was built. Black Hawk looked up and saw the balcony sliding down towards him, and it seemed as though the rooms on the passage beyond were suddenly opening and spilling their contents upon them.

He shouted, 'Run!' And he leapt like lightning for the outer door. The American was slower, and he got caught, and went down with a beam across his shoulders. Black Hawk could see that he was dazed but not seriously hurt, and he rushed back and heaved mightily and threw the beam away. And then he picked up the American and ran out into the sunshine with him.

The defenders of the wall were looking towards the fortress at that moment. The northern end, where the flagstaff was, hadn't suffered so much in the bombardment, and now two men were running on to its flat roof to bring down the flag of Spain.

Fortress Santa Maria was surrendering to the gringo enemy.

Because of their interest in that descending flag, the Spaniards and their Indian allies along the ramparts failed to see the pair who came staggering from that drunken, collapsing building.

Black Hawk felt the American stir and then he heard that nasal voice say: 'Put me down, brother. I can still walk.'

Black Hawk set him on his feet, and then supported him until he had the use of his legs. And then they looked around for a way of escape, and there seemed none.

For at that moment Spanish defenders, who had no heart for battle anyway, went running across to the gate to lift up the mighty wooden bars which kept it shuttered against assault. They saw the gates begin to swing open, while a deputation of Spaniards formed up to go out and parley with the enemy.

And through those opening gates, Black Hawk saw the American cavalry trotting forward to take possession of this fortress.

They semed to have got out of the prison too late to save themselves! Now, within seconds, the Americans would be taking possession of Fortress Santa Maria, and these Americanos were much more efficient than the Spaniards, and once they were in possession of this town there would be no escaping from it.

The Indian and his American friend looked at each other, and their eyes were startled. Black Hawk heard the American exclaim. 'What on earth do we do now, Black Hawk?'

Black Hawk hesitated. And then he saw Indians pouring off the ramparts in wild confusion, and racing down towards the harbour. He shouted: 'Come on, white man!' and in his excitement he spoke in his own language, but the American understood, and the two began to run with the tide of frantic, panicking Indians. No one gave a thought to them. Every Indian's mind was concerned at this moment with escape from the dreaded American with anything valuable they could salvage from their huts. For they knew that the Americans were often abrupt in their treatment of Indian prisoners.

Black Hawk and the American ran down among the huts, but Black Hawk was leading the way, and he dodged behind the reed huts until he came to that place under the ramparts where he could see the leafy top of that fallen elm which had been a ladder to freedom for the remnants of the Cherokee tribe.

His quick eyes darted round, to see some way of clambering up the wall at this point. There were no soldiers here now, all having crowded towards the main gates with the cessation of hostilities.

Black Hawk took a leap and caught the protruding

end of a roof beam of one of the reed huts. It was flimsy and seemed unlikely to bear his weight, but he knew better. He pulled himself up and sat on the thatched roof, and then carefully he straightened so that he was standing on a beam support. His eyes measured the distance across to the rampart that must have killed thousands of its slave builders. Then he leapt across space and his fingers found a hand-hold, and then he pulled himself up on to the firing platform behind the castellations.

Then he lay on his stomach, and put his hands over the edge of the wall, and at once the American divined what was in his mind.

The American went back among the huts to take a run at the hands extended to help him. It was unfortunate for him that he went so far back, because an Indian, coming out of his hut, suddenly saw the hated blue uniform. He must have thought that the enemy were quickly in amongst them, and he dropped his possessions and strung an arrow to his bow.

The American didn't see the action and started to run forward. He was just leaping through the air, when an arrow bit into his shoulder.

Black Hawk saw the spasm of pain that twisted that American's red, perspiring face, and then he saw the eyes seemed to glaze, and the head dropped and then the body went limp.

But in that fraction of a second Black Hawk's hands stabbed out and caught the hands of the stricken American. And then the full weight of that heavy body was dependent upon Black Hawk's arms, lying there with his body half over the rampart.

He took the strain, and through the sweat that ran into his eyes he looked quickly over that sunlit town and harbour. He saw Indians fleeing by boat, but the Spaniards were marching back up to the main gate in attitudes of surrender.

Black Hawk lay a few seconds to get his strength back. And then he began a mighty display of his physical powers.

He began to lift that dead weight by the sheer strength of his enormous biceps. And then, when the unconscious American's head was level with his own, the Indian began to pull his knees up under him, and then to stand erect, at the same time bringing the American up from the depths with him.

With a final mighty effort he pulled the American on to the rampart, and then he collapsed against the wall, the strength drained out of him by that herculean effort.

But again there was no time for Black Hawk to lie where he was.

When he lifted his head and looked towards the main gate, he saw the cavalry riding in and rounding up the Spanish prisoners who were standing with their hands above their heads. And infantry were running to take up strategic positions, some even beginning to climb to the rampart where they could look over the town. Yet others were racing down the cobbled roadway into the town, and plainly they were ripe for loot and murder and mischief.

Black Hawk rolled over to look at his companion. There was a fluttering to those eyes which betokened a return to consciousnes. Gently but swiftly Black Hawk snapped off the feathered end to that protruding shaft, and then seized the flint arrowhead which protruded through the American's fleshy underarm, and then pulled and the arrow came clean through. There was no time to bandage the wound.

Black Hawk stood over the American and then hoisted him on to his shoulder and then, as if the tiredness had gone completely from that mighty, muscular body, the Indian clambered into a recess in the wall where the fallen tree lay crotched. He began the descent of that tree which was as easy as a ladder to negotiate when a man was unencumbered, but was suddenly treacherous and uncertain with this great weight on his back.

When he was a few yards down the trunk, he had to pause because the American was returning to consciousness and struggling. Black Hawk grunted for him to keep still or they would both fall off the tree and break their necks, and the American was reassured by his voice and did as he was told.

In that pause Black Hawk looked out over the great plain which went westwards as far as his eye could see. He saw the main mass of American soldiery grouped where the cannons were being brought out of action and taken towards the open fortress gates. And then he saw the movement of other troops across the plain, and he stiffened, his eyes watching them and seeing a significance in their movement.

He saw a long column of infantry moving rapidly towards the south, and there was a caution in the way they went through the many bushes that covered this plain, which told him a story immediately.

His people had been seen! The fleeing Cherokees were in deadly danger. Now that the fortress had fallen, strong forces of infantry had been despatched to round up the unfortunate Indians.

And then Black Hawk caught a glimpse of the Cherokees. They had taken shelter in a valley about a mile away. He could see them crowding there, and the thought came to him immediately. 'They do not know that the American soldiers are stealing up on them!' They would be lying there, resting and hiding, when suddenly that big force of blue-shirted Americans would descend upon them.

12

THE RESCUE

Black Hawk went down the rest of that tree trunk as if he had no burden upon his shoulders. He had to get to his people and warn them of the danger before they were surrounded and shot down or taken prisoner.

When he was on the ground he stood the American on his feet. He told the American, 'My people are in danger. I must leave you because there are many lives I must save now.'

The newspaper man swayed on his feet, but there was a smile on his red, perspiring face. He said drily, 'Looks like you make a habit of saving people's lives, O Black Hawk.'

The American put out his hand. Black Hawk took it and they shook hands clasped in Indian fashion.

The American said, simply. 'Meeting you confirms what I've always thought about Injuns. There's good

146

and bad in every race, and it's wrong to treat you as General Jackson has treated you Cherokees. If you can escape with your lives now, Black Hawk, you will find friends in the north rallying to help you. You can leave me now. I'll keep out of the hands of Spanish, Injuns and Americans, and I'll get back to my paper and report about this Florida incident.'

No more was said. There was not time for more. Black Hawk looked into that face and knew he had a friend for life.

He turned and loped into the bushes. When he turned again, that big blue-shirted American newspaper man had disappeared. Black Hawk felt satisfied. Somehow that resourceful newspaper man would get news of this foray back to his newspaper in the north.

He put his head down, his eyes looked for tracks of his people. They were easy to read. He went along the trail as fast as he could go, and he went recklessly, without thought for his own safety.

Luck was with him. Just in time, he saw movement ahead through the bushes, and he recognized the blue shirts of the enemy.

They were already closing in on his people, were already ringing them round. Black Hawk halted in his tracks, standing in the cover of a tall, flowering bush. Desperately his brown eyes searched on either side of him. He realized that the American infantry was stationary – they had been put into position and were obviously now awaiting some signal to advance.

147

Probably within minutes it would come, just as soon as other troops were in position.

Black Hawk glided forward like a great brown cat. He discarded his rifle now, because he knew this was a moment for stealth.

And then luck was with him. He stepped out from a bush unexpectedly into a clearing where an officer sat on a white horse. The officer had a whistle to his lips, and was holding a watch in his hand. As Black Hawk looked he saw a movement, as if the officer were about to pocket that watch. Black Hawk sensed that the moment that was done, that whistle would blow and the column would fall upon the Indians lying up in that valley beyond.

Black Hawk began to run forward. And then, yards from the rear of that horse, he took off in a mighty leap which landed him right behind the officer in the saddle. The officer never blew that whistle. An arm crooked around his throat, and he felt himself falling from the saddle. They hit the earth with an almighty bump, and then the struggles of the officer ceased as Black Hawk rendered him unconscious.

Black Hawk rose when he had silenced the man who had been about to send troops on to his people. Panting he glared round, and then realized that the incident had been so swift and silent that no one had heard it. All the infantry were a couple of dozen yards or more ahead, and screened by the thick undergrowth.

Black Hawk went through that line of crouching

soldiers. There were soldiers at intervals of less than ten yards apart, and yet that Indian glided past them and there was not a man who saw him go.

He kept low, crawling on his belly at times, but at all times progressing swiftly, in the manner of an Indian born to the trail. And when he felt himself far enough ahead to be screened by intervening bushes and he got to his feet and ran forward.

Within yards he came upon one of the few Cherokee sentries that were on watch. The brave hadn't seen any suspicious movement on the part of the infantry, and when he saw Black Hawk leaping towards him his mouth opened to give a cry of delight. Black Hawk stopped the cry before it could betray them.

A surprised sentry found a hand clasped across his mouth, and he heard Black Hawk hissing into his ear, 'Silence! Let us go, for the American soldiers are about to descend upon us!'

He ran on at that and the other brave followed, and suddenly they came down a bush-covered slope and ran into the tiny wooded valley in which the Cherokee survivors were resting.

There were glad cries from those weary, resting Indian men, women and children, for Black Hawk was a favourite among the tribe. His eyes sought for Lone Fern, and he saw her standing apart from the others, and though she did not come towards him he knew that she was glad to see him again. He knew that her heart was beating faster, and he could see the shine in her eyes, and the flush that came to that lovely maiden's face.

He turned away from Lone Fern, satisfied, now that he had seen her again. There were important things to be done in the next few minutes and there was no time for looking at each other.

The tribe's people were suddenly hushed as they saw that mighty warrior waving imperiously to call in the men of the tribe for a talk. They recognized in that instant that they were not yet safe.

Black Hawk made a brief speech to the handful of men who came and stood before him.

'This is no place to rest in,' he told them. 'The American soldiers know that you are in this valley, and now that they have taken the fortress they have moved troops down to encircle you in order to launch an attack on you.'

There were quick little cries of fear from the exhausted women with their children on the fringe of those proud, silent braves. But Black Hawk went on without heeding them.

'Even now they are waiting for a signal to begin the attack, but that signal will not be given for some time.' Not until that officer returned to consciousness, or his lieutenants discovered him lying there, Black Hawk thought. But he didn't say anything of this to his people. 'We must steal away quickly, and try to escape before they begin to close in on this valley,' he urged.

He spoke bravely and he did not let them see what

150

was in his heart. For as he looked round at those tired people, at the old and the overburdened and the lame, he knew that their pace must be so slow that inevitably they must be overtaken.

But it was not in Black Hawk's mind to stay there and be overrun and perhaps wiped out by these victory-intoxicated blueshirts. While there was breath in his body, he would try to save himself and his people.

The braves marshalled the people into line again, and now that they had rested for an hour they were better able to resume the march. Black Hawk raced ahead followed by a few of the unwounded braves, while the rest of the menfolk took up protective positions on the flank of the refugees.

Black Hawk went swiftly and silently to the head of the valley, and then he climbed a tree and scanned the bushcovered plain ahead of him.

He realized then that the American troops had been drawn up in two parallel lines along the summit of the hills between which that tiny, winding, wooded valley ran. He could see blueshirts lying behind cover on cither side of him, but he realized that the end of the valley was still open.

He dropped to the ground, and urged his people to come along quickly and silently, and then, while the American soldiers lay and waited for a signal to pour down the valley sides on to the hapless Cherokees, Black Hawk began to lead his people to safety right from under their very noses.

They walked in fear, and if a baby had cried out their lives would have been forfeit in an instant. They went swiftly, silently, their hearts in their mouths, and every moment they expected to see blue-shirted men with rifles rising from the bushes on either side of them to pour a deadly hail of lead into their weary ranks.

And yet nothing of the kind happened. Skilfully led by Black Hawk, they climbed a narrow deer trail that went through the narrowing valley end and then over a small hill on to the more level plain beyond.

Black Hawk and his braves stood aside in the most dangerous part, where the people poured through that gap at the end of the valley. They waited with hands on their weapons and eyes turned outwards from their people to catch the first glimpse of danger.

The last of the people were just going over that wooded brow, when in the distance Black Hawk's sharp ears heard a shout of fury.

Either that officer had recovered, or the soldiers had discovered what had been done to him!

Now Black Hawk urged his people into top speed because though they were out of the trap the danger from pursuit was just as deadly. He and his men fell to the rear of that stumbling, fleeing column of help-less people, and they faced backwards, ready to give their lives to save their people.

And now they were going on to a part of the plain

where there was less cover, and inevitably that meant they were seen.

A mighty roaring sound, like the angry buzz of bees at a disturbed hive, arose from the tiny hills above that valley that was to have been the death-bed for the Cherokee survivors. They had been seen and now the pursuit was on.

The infantry came recklessly in pursuit, sure that they could deal with this almost harmless body of Indians. Their recklessness proved expensive to them.

They found themselves faced by a resolute rearguard of Cherokees under Black Hawk, who used every inch of cover to protect themselves, and strung death-dealing shafts at the blue-shirted infantry as they came charging into view across the plain.

There was a fight of incredible savagery, with that rearguard tenaciously holding the enemy from their people. For half an hour that mad, headlong flight went on across the nearly-open plain, and never once did that gallant rearguard of Indians allow the infantry to come within rifle range of their helpless people. The infantry learned its lesson, and grouped and came on more cautiously, and now Black Hawk's warriors began to suffer because of those accurate soldiers' rifles.

Then, on the side of a sloping mound that was bare of cover, those Cherokee people sank to the ground, unable to continue their flight any longer. It was more than flesh and blood could stand after all

they had endured. If this was to be the end, then it
had to be. They huddled together in a frightened,
exhausted group, the women with their children,
and the brave old men standing like shields around
them. And out beyond them, Black Hawk and his
dwindling band of warriors fought tenaciously
against an enemy twenty times their number, and
being reinforced every minute. They were creeping
closer now, intent on getting within range of those
people on the bare hillside.

And Black Hawk knew there was nothing that
could stop them. He fought on, but he thought,
'This is useless. It is a question now of minutes before
our long journey comes to an end.'

Yet still he encouraged his warriors and recklessly
exposed himself to danger whenever it was necessary
to hold back the more impetuous of the opposing
infantry.

He saw the infantry lining up, and he knew that
this was preparatory to a final charge that would over-
run his few men and carry the infantry on to
surround and capture those who remained alive of
his people. He even saw a sergeant with a whistle to
his lips, just as that officer's had been, back beyond
the valley.

This time there was no means of stopping that
signal for the assault. The whistle blew, and these
blue shirted infantry rose in a mighty, all swamping
wave and began to crash towards the remnants of the
Cherokee tribe.

It was the end . . .

It wasn't the end!

Black Hawk, sweat streaming down his face from his exertions, and still fighting back at these men who menaced his people, heard shrill cries of his womenfolk on the hillside, and there was gladness in their voices.

He turned, astonished that he should hear that sound, and then he saw a sight that made the hair stand on his head, and the blood tingle in his veins.

For all along the summit of that bare sloping mound was a mighty throng of mounted Indians. As he looked there was the wild war-cry of Creek and Seminole braves, and then they came down that hillside in a flurry of flying manes and tossing war plumes, with feathered lances raised aloft, and guns banging and bows sending a cloud of arrows towards the halted infantrymen.

The sight of that horde had brought the infantry's attack to a complete halt. They weren't even firing now, they were so amazed to see such a throng so unexpectedly out there on that great plain.

Black Hawk shouted to his warriors to fall back, and they raced to where their people were. From the heights of that slope he could look behind, and he saw cavalry coming from the distant fortress to reinforce the infantry, and he knew that the approach of the Creek and Seminoles had been detected by General Jackson's troops within the fortress. He realized, too, that though the Creek and Seminole rescuers were in force, if a battle were pitched between them and the better-armed Americans, the Indians would suffer annihilation just as the Cherokees had done.

He saw a Creek chief through the swirling dust clouds as those Indian horsemen raced down and around the Cherokees, and he shouted, 'Go back! You cannot fight and win against these Americans!'

And perhaps that was in the minds of these Creek and Seminole chiefs, for while some raced alongside the kneeling American infantry and held them back, the rest swung round and each began to pick up a woman or a child or one of the wounded or aged Cherokee males.

Within seconds – in a miraculously short space of time – every Cherokee was lifted off the ground, and was being borne in a thunderous passage westwards towards the safety of the Creek and Seminole country. And then the rescuing Indians pulled away from their fight with the infantry, just in time to avoid the ponderous charge of American cavalry. They came triumphantly racing upon the heels of their over-burdened brothers.

There was no fight after that. The Indians rode westwards and then halted to make the Cherokees more comfortable on the horses. There were glad greetings and the chiefs all came and spoke to the refugees who had come so far – and had now found safety.

One of them told Black Hawk, 'A white man rode

into our camp during the the night. He was a brave man and risked his life to do so. He told us of your peril . . .'

The British secret agent had been able to help the Cherokees yet again . . .

Lone Fern was waiting for her warrior when they rode into the Indian's camp. Side by side they went in among the tepees, and when people looked upon the young couple they knew they were mates.